.

# True Control 4.1

**Books by Willow Madison**

True Nature

True Beginnings

True Choices

True Control 4.2

we were one once 1

we were one once 2

Existential Angst

the SAYER

# True Control 4.1


# Willow Madison

Madison, Willow

True Control (True Series, Book Four . One)

Front Cover Design by David Colon (www.colonfilm.com); Back Cover Design by XIX (www.thenineteen.net)

This is a work of fiction. Names, characters, places and incidents are either the product of the author's imagination or are used fictitiously, and any resemblance to actual persons, living or dead, business establishments, events or locales is entirely coincidental.

This book is intended for adults only. Spanking and other sexual activities represented in this book are fantasies only, intended for adults. Nothing in the book should be interpreted as advocating any non-consensual spanking activity or the spanking of minors.

www.willowmadisonbooks.com

ISBN-13: 978-0-9963191-4-0
ISBN-10: 0-9963191-4-X

## 1 Him

"Mr. Traeger, we just need to go over this one more time." The short detective is taking a seat at my table across from me. I didn't tell him he could. I've given up control of my apartment, my car, my office.

The other detectives are standing in a group near my terrace doors, staying out of the way of the people working around my living room. They've already finished with the other rooms. I haven't talked to this detective yet. He just stood in the background up until now.

With my head in my hands still, I growl, "I've been over this and over this." I look up, my bloodshot eyes bouncing around the room full of cops. "When are you people going to tell *me* something?!" Jeff puts his hand on my shoulder to try to calm me, but this only angers me more. I stand up quickly and go to the kitchen.

Jake is leaning against the counter. He shakes his head and hands me a small scotch. I shouldn't be drinking, not now, but I need to calm my nerves.

Jeff comes in and says quietly, "Max, you need to cooperate. I know this is frustrating, but this is how it works. This *is* how we'll find Lucy." *I know he's right.* He got the ball moving fast on this, calling in favors from his cop days. I take another gulp and put the glass down, a little calmer. I walk back to the dining table and sit down.

"Max!" Dad pushes past two cops by the door and rushes to me. I smile slightly, seeing his look of shock and anger, I know it mirrors my own. My brother's been trying to stay calm and neutral for my sake, but Dad isn't one to hide his feelings behind a mask.

"Where's Mom?"

"Jake said it was a zoo here. I thought it'd be best if she comes later. When we get this place cleared out."

"Good." I turn to the detective again. Taking a deep breath, "Where do you want me to start?"

"You said the last time you saw or spoke to your wife was when you left after lunch," he refers to his notes, "about 1:00?"

"Yes. We had lunch together here. Lucy had an appointment with her doctor at 2:00. Jeff drove me to my client meetings in the afternoon." I say this last part through gritted teeth. I still blame myself for not having Jeff drive her. I had too many appointments all over town today; I needed him to keep me on schedule.

"Sorry to interrupt, Det. Killaney. We have everything we need here." The detective nods to the uniformed cops and watches as most of the people leave my apartment. *It's a mess of dust and prints and tossed shit everywhere*. They've searched every inch of the apartment looking for any sign of a struggle or hint where Lucy could be. I didn't think they'd find anything here, but I let them loose to do what they needed to do. *My car and office must look the same*.

"And that was with her OB/GYN doctor," again back to the notes, "Dr. Patel?"

"Yes. Her office left a message that Lucy missed the appointment." I'm starting to go numb giving these details again. *It's either go numb or go ballistic*.

"I got three."

"What?" Through my numbness, I frown at him.

"Three kids. Three boys. Have you been trying long?"

"No." I don't want to answer questions about this. It's too painful to think about Lucy missing and possibly pregnant too.

The detective leans in a little to look at my face more closely. "Ya know it takes some couples a long time to get pregnant. My wife and I were lucky; well, if you call having three boys in less than four years lucky."

I know he's pushing me, to get me out of my numbness, but I'm drained. Dad isn't, he reacts quickly. "Detective, can I ask what the hell that has to do with anything? Or how that helps find my daughter-in-law?"

The detective looks up slowly at my dad and I follow his eyes up too. Dad has his stern "lawyer pushing a client to do what he says look" that I've seen so often. I can see Jake standing with Jeff in the background, both tense. "Sir. Can I get your name for the record?"

"Ronald Traeger. Now answer my question, Detective."

"I'm trying to help your son to remember as much detail as he can." He looks at me, his eyes narrowing, taking in my slumped shoulders and broken state. "I think he's at his limit though in answering questions tonight."

"No. I want to get through this. Go on. Ask what you need to." I'm still numb though. Killaney raises his eyebrows, but goes back to his notepad.

"So when you didn't hear from your wife this afternoon, you tracked her phone?"

"No. I assumed Lucy was busy with her chores. I tracked her phone when I got home and found she wasn't here and wasn't answering my calls or texts."

He picks up the baggie that has the list of chores I'd left for Lucy this morning. "And this is your handwriting; this is a list of *chores* for your wife?"

"Yes."

"And you do this, leave a similar list, each morning?" I can see yesterday's list in a ball in another bag. They must've pulled it from the trash.

"Yes." I can feel Dad tensing behind me, his hand is on the back of my chair.

Det. Killaney continues holding the bag, but changes directions in questions, "But you didn't just track the GPS, you were able to check her calls and messages too?"

"Yes. I have an app that allows me to check her calls, texts, voicemail and GPS."

"And you often check these things…your wife's calls and messages?" He says this quietly, looking down at his notes before bringing his eyes to stare into mine, sizing me up again.

"Not often."

"What? Every day, every other day, once a week…?"

"Usually only if she leaves the house."

"So, what happens if Lucy doesn't get through her chores?" He's appraising me again.

*I knew this would come up. So far, it hadn't, but this must be the 'bad cop.'*

Dad butts in, "I think Max does need a break, Detective."

I don't take my eyes off Killaney. "Dad. It's fine. I need them to get through eliminating me as a suspect as quickly as possible to focus on what happened to Lucy."

"Why would I think you're a suspect, Max?" Killaney's stare is alert again, but he keeps his body purposefully relaxed.

"Isn't the husband always the first one?"

He laughs, "Usually. But you seem awfully calm about that…"

I only shrug. Jeff had talked me through all this on the drive back to my apartment and while waiting for everyone to show up. Eventually, all the details of my marriage with Lucy will come to light if the investigation goes on. *God. If my Lucy isn't found.*

I lower my head at this thought. *My Lucy. Where are you, little girl?*

"So…what happens?" I look dumbly up at him, so he spells it out for me, "What happens if your wife doesn't finish the chores you've given her, Max?"

I answer calmly, from a tunnel in my head, "It depends on the chore, on her excuse."

He picks up the list and reads, "Run two miles in under thirty-five minutes. What if she didn't get this one done?"

"I crossed it off the list. Lucy wasn't feeling well this morning again."

"Hmmm…morning sickness or something else?"

I narrow my eyes again, even in my haze I don't like discussing this. "I don't know."

"So…what about this one; it's not crossed off." He points towards the bottom of the list. "What if Lucy didn't get your suit from the dry cleaners, Max? What would happen?"

"She didn't."

"What?"

"She didn't get to most of those chores today. The dry cleaning would've been hanging in the front of the closet if she had."

"And when you got home, you checked?"

"Not right away. I checked when Jeff and I got back here. While we waited."

"Hmmm…and what were you going to do if Lucy walked in the door while you were waiting…with all these chores undone?" He's quiet, calm, like we're discussing the weather instead of my missing wife.

Dad clears his throat. "I think that's enough questions, son."

"I would've punished her." I take some satisfaction in seeing the cop's eyebrows lift in surprise. He wasn't expecting me to be so blunt.

"I'm afraid I'm going to have to ask you to elaborate, Max." He lifts his eyes in warning to Dad.

## 2 Her

The smell is the first thing to hit me. That and something metal as my body is bounced around.

I realize I'm on my side. And I can't move. *Oh, God. I can't move my arms or legs*! I panic, screaming against something on my mouth, pushing with all my might against whatever is holding my arms and legs together. I finally stop, the strain is too much. I breathe quickly, but only through my nose.

I push my tongue forward; it sticks a little. *Tape? I have tape over my mouth*? This chills me. I stop moving. I pull in and out quick snotty breaths through my nose. I move and stretch my face, tearing painfully against the stickiness, trying to loosen it. A corner finally starts to come up. *Good*. I rub this against the smelly carpet or whatever that is. A side comes off. I turn my head and gulp air. I get the rest to roll off and try to breathe normally.

I try to think. *I have to think*. I focus on what I know, what I think I know. Ignore what I can't figure out. *Concentrate.* It's Max's voice that I hear in my head.

*I'm in a car*? I can hear the engine, smell the gas. My eyes can't adjust to the light. *Okay. That was a curve and rough road*. My body is knocked around, the wheels below me thumping hard against the road, my hips and shoulders pushed painfully against metal. *I must be in the trunk of something*.

*I hear music...barely. Country music*. I don't recognize it, but it's twangy. And I hear gravel and dirt crunching below wheels. *We've slowed down.*

I panic thinking for a moment...*who's driving?! Who's we?! No...No...think only about what I can know*. I breathe. I try screaming, but the music just gets louder. I stop, my throat is already raw.

*My legs and arms are tied. My mouth was taped. I'm in a trunk. On a dirt road*. I repeat this like lyrics to the twangy music.

My head hurts, pounds. The faint taste of something chemical mixes with the smell of moldy carpet, gas, and metal. *I was drugged*. I fight back the urge to vomit, the motion of the car not helping. I have to breathe and concentrate on the music to get the feeling under control. I laugh hysterically for a moment. *God help me if I get vomit all over myself*. It takes longer to breathe this hysteria away.

I vaguely remember stumbling on the street and being pulled to a curb...*was that a dream*?

3 Him

"My son won't be elaborating on anything, Detective." Dad steps around to stand slightly between my chair and the table.

"Dad…"

"I'm going to have to insist after that answer that your son give me some details."

"Dad. Sir." He turns to me at the commanding tone I use; it's the same one Lucy would've responded to. *I may be in a fog, but I can see only one thing clearly. Lucy is gone and I need her back*. "Dad, no stone will be left unturned and I won't delay the police looking for what really happened with Lucy today."

He nods once, but doesn't move away, only turns to give Killaney a clear look at me.

I sit up straighter, clearing my head with a shake. "Please. Detective Killaney…?"

"You were about to tell me how you *punish* your wife, Mr. Traeger…" His short round body is leaning forward in the chair, his feet just touching the ground.

I take a deep breath. "My wife and I have an unusual relationship. Unusual in today's standards anyway." I pause and look at my hands. They itch to have Lucy here, under them. *What I wouldn't give to be angry at her for only forgetting to do the dishes earlier*. I look back into the cop's eyes. "I set rules. Lucy follows them. I set consequences. Lucy submits to them."

"What kind of consequences…?"

I square my shoulders and speak slowly. I don't want to show any anger or fear. I need to get the police beyond looking at me and to start looking for what really happened. "I will spank my wife, ground her, take away phone and other privileges. Slap her. Anything short of beating her with my fists or a heavy solid object." Even I'm surprised at how succinctly I can explain this. *I'm a monster in my rages against her, but it sounds…natural when said like this, out loud.*

He laughs, a short, quick laugh with a shake of his head, "Well…Mr. Traeger…" He exhales with a laugh again, a sigh, "I've never heard a husband try to convince me he's innocent in his wife's disappearance in quite this way…" He stops shaking his head, all amusement gone. He just waits for my reply.

"What else do you want to know, Detective?"

"Well, for starters we'll go back over all the details of yesterday. That was the last day that your wife's whereabouts can be confirmed by anyone other than you…" *Bad cop has hit his stride now.*

I sit back. *I can only hope this goes quickly. And that other detectives are figuring out where my Lucy is in the meantime.* "Fine. But I need assurances." Dad turns to squeeze my shoulder. He's been quiet, but I can see his emotions playing across his face. He's been angry along with me.

"Like what?"

"I need your assurance that I'm not wasting my time here. That there's a full force of police out looking beyond the door of my apartment for Lucy. Because I know my wife isn't here. I need assurances that you're not just fucking with me to make a report and then disappear while my Lucy is out there somewhere. Fucking lost." I try for an even voice, but I lose it a little saying her name. I bury my fear in calm anger. "I need to know, Det. Killaney, that every Goddamn thing is being done to look for my wife while I sit here with you."

I see Jeff move closer to the table. He shares a nod with the detective but doesn't say anything.

Dad turns to me and whispers in my ear, "I'll call my contact in the Mayor's office again." I nod at him and he walks towards the kitchen.

"Of course, Mr. Traeger. We're doing everything to find Lucy. And your cooperation is helping a great deal. Any information you can provide will help, will lead to finding her." He appraises me though. *He's not convinced…yet anyway...that I'm not a suspect*. I breathe in and out quickly. *Goddammit*!

"Have you checked the building's security videos yet?" Jeff speaks up behind me.

Killaney glances up at him, but answers looking at me. "Yes. All are fuzzy like most of them. Poor camera quality, only 48 hours kept recorded."

"And?" Jeff sounds angry. He takes a breath. I've tried to teach him to control his anger, but he has a long way to go.

I take over asking, "Did you see Lucy on today's tape, coming or going? Or anyone on our floor?"

"We saw a person get into the elevator on the penthouse level around 1:30 today, alone. We saw what looks like the same person leave the elevator and building shortly after." *A good legalese maneuver. No commitment to anything.*

"And was this person about five feet, with long blond curls, in a dress or skirt, with a purse similar to the one found today?" I lean forward to ask; I desperately want to know for sure that Lucy left here on her own.

"That meets the description of the person, but we can't confirm that it's your wife. The image is unclear for now." Killaney stops and pulls up a new sheet of notes; he's dramatically slow. "We do however show a man meeting your description coming and going on the penthouse level between 10:30 a.m. and 11:15 a.m. today." He glances at his watch, "Yesterday now. Can you confirm your whereabouts at that time, Max?"

Jeff starts to speak up before me, "I was driving Max to an appointment about…" but the Detective's eyes aren't on him.

Jake moves closer to the table, "That was me." Killaney leans back, looking between Jake and me.

"You were here today? You saw Lucy?" The wind is knocked from my words.

"And for the record…you're Jake Traeger?" Killaney writes this down as Jake nods in response. Jake doesn't take his eyes from me; his face is still a mask. But Killaney picks up my question, "So you saw Lucy today, yesterday..." He corrects himself again, "in this apartment?"

"Yes."

## 4 Her

I hear a door screech open, the car rocks slightly with the movement of the driver getting out, my bruised elbow hits against the worn carpet and metal floor again. The car door slams closed, my startled scream mixes with the loud bang. I hear footsteps crunch, slide on the gravel. *Oh God Oh God Oh God...please...no*. I squeeze my eyes shut and strain against the restraints.

*No. Keep your eyes open.*

It's Max again in my head, his deep commanding voice I've come to crave. And I obey it as I always do.

I hear a beeping and pop of the trunk door. Dull starlight, cold air, wooded smells hit me. I start screaming right before a large fist connects with my cheek and the stars fade...

5 Him

"What were you doing here, Jake?" My voice isn't my own. *I can't be this calm and this angry. Is this what insanity sounds like*? He only stares at me. I see to my side that Jeff has moved to stand slightly in between us, but is staring in disbelief at my brother too.

Killaney interrupts, "Why didn't you come forward with this information earlier?"

Jake turns his attention from me to the cop. "I didn't think it mattered."

Now Killaney is staring in disbelief, with a little laugh, "You didn't think it would matter? O. K." He takes a breath. "Have a seat." He points to the other side of the table from me. Jeff moves in this direction following Jake, keeping between us still.

Jake won't make eye contact with me. Killaney starts a new sheet of notes, but I can tell that he's taking notice of my slowly heating anger. I've wanted to hit something all night and Jake's face is looking pretty good for it.

"So…you arrived in this apartment about 10:30 a.m. yesterday?"

"Yes."

"Lucy answered the door?"

"Yes."

"How did she seem then?"

Jake frowns, his mask of neutrality lost for a second. He blinks it back into place. *My little brother, the emotional one. He's calm?* "Lucy seemed fine."

"Fine? What else?"

He pauses again. "She was happy to see me." He looks down at his clasped hands on the table to avoid seeing my reaction.

"Do you see…" Killaney glances at me and shifts in his seat a little, not finishing his question. "Was there anyone else here?"

"No."

"Did she mention where she was going in the afternoon?"

"Yes. Her doctor," Jake glances briefly in my direction, "and errands."

"Her list of chores?" Killaney is sarcastic. *I wish I could punch him too*. I take a few deep silent breaths to get under control again.

"Yes." Jake's voice takes on a little edge.

"Were you just in the neighborhood…?"

"No. I came here to see Lucy." *Damn*. I put my hands under the table to hide my fists.

"Was Lucy expecting you?"

"Yes." Jeff moves a little closer. I freeze with my fists clenched as much as my jaw. *I can't believe what I'm hearing!*

## 6 Her

I try to move my head and feel a cold, damp cloth against the right side of my face, scratching against my cheek. My head bounces a little and I vomit.

"Fuck!" *A man's voice…a voice I don't know*. I'm thrown hard to dirt and gravel, unable to break my fall, my body still tied. My cry is weak. "You're gonna pay for that!"

*I remember now. I'm bound. But I'm out of the car*. I listen to the scream coming from my left cheek and leave my head against the dirt. I can't move. I open my right eye just as something is thrown over my face.

The smell of the damp cloth and my own vomit is overpowering. I vomit a little again, right onto the dirt not even lifting my head.

"Stop that!" A kick to my thigh accompanies this. I try to curl up more, but can't hardly bring my legs up.

A hand rips off the cloth and grabs my head up, another grabs my shoulder and yanks me a foot; some hair pulls loose. I scream until I'm dropped again.

I hear his footsteps crunch away from me. They clump up wooden steps. *One two three four*. They clump across more wood. *One two*.

Keys rattle together, against wood. A door bangs open. I jump against the dirt. I'm hiccupping, trying to get control of my breathing. I turn my head. *Breathe. Don't you dare vomit! Breathe!* Max's voice helps.

I open my eyes. *No. I open my right eye*. My left isn't listening to me. A weak light is behind me. I see the front of the car I must've been in. I'm lying on a dirt and gravel drive. I can't see beyond into the darkness.

I'm lifted roughly up, my left cheek banging against damp skin. I cry out, squeezing my right eye shut. "You vomit on me again, bitch, and I'll shove it down your throat."

I open my right eye, but can't see his face. I wildly look around, can't focus. *Focus! I'm trying, Max…really I am. Why don't you tell him to stop banging my head?!* I almost laugh. *You're getting hysterical, baby.*

I open my right eye again just as I pass through the wood door I heard open. He spins around quickly and it takes all the strength I have not to throw up. I'm dropped onto something cushioned. I bounce but keep my stomach down. *Good girl.*

## 7 Him

"Do you see your sister-in-law alone often?" Killaney is keeping his eyes on me as he questions Jake now.

"Not often." Jake's voice is still even. With the detective no longer watching him, he turns his eyes to me. I can't read his face. *Pain? Guilt? Anger*?

"What's not often?"

"Once a week." I keep my expression impassive, but my hands clench and unclench under the table. *I didn't know this. How did I not know this?*

Killaney pauses to look between us. I don't take my eyes off my brother. I don't even move when Dad comes back in and stops behind Jake.

"So…you come over *here* every time or…?" It's a quiet question. Killaney's trying to keep everything calm with his tone.

"Yes."

"Same day each week?"

"Yes." I see Dad's eyes turning from questioning to stern above Jake's head, but I still keep my stare on my brother.

"Yesterday?" Jake only nods. "So, every Friday you come here to see Lucy?" Jake nods again. "Same time?"

"Yes."

I know why before Killaney asks him. "Because Max has a set staff meeting."

The detective sits back. I don't wait for him to ask anything else.

I lean forward, only a little, my voice is edged glass. "How long was this going on, Jake?"

He shakes his head in the slightest way and looks at Killaney quickly before meeting my eyes again. "Only a little while."

"So why were you seeing my wife every week, Jake, without my knowledge?"

But Killaney breaks in with his own question, "What's a little while? Weeks, months?"

Jake tears his eyes from mine, but doesn't meet Killaney's. He looks at his hands instead. "It's been a few months."

"How'd it start?"

Jake again shakes his head and keeps his eyes lowered at Killaney's question. He finally lifts his head and looks at me once more. "The first time was after we picked Lucy up from that Italian place near where she worked."

I get the looks now. Jake's trying to warn me against pushing him to answer in front of the police. *This is why he didn't say he was here.*

Because that was the night I beat Lucy pretty badly with the belt. *But that still doesn't explain why Jake has been coming over when he knows I'm not here. To see my Lucy. And it's been going on for months.*

8 Her

My right eye is pressed against a scratchy sofa. It's covered in wet-dog smelling hair. My knees press into its back. I can't open my left eye at all. Even trying to pushes the throbbing aside for shooting stars of head-ripping pain. I breathe, trying to listen. *Focus, baby.*

And I'm chilled to hear something familiar.

A leather belt being pulled slowly out of pants inches above me.

The whoosh and strike, together with my scream, fill my head with a new pain. The belt doesn't stop hitting me, everywhere, my legs, arms, feet, hands, butt, back. The belt licks at every inch of me. I bury my face in the cushion to try to protect the only thing I can. The belt hits my head, my ear. I scream in and out the nasty hair stuck to the cushion.

He stops. I'm a bound ball of fire. I don't hear him move. I don't see him. I try to calm myself quickly, to swallow my cries and ignore the pain.

He grabs around my waist with one arm. I catch a glimpse of dark hair, a white tank top, strong arms. That's it. He carries me around the sofa and tosses me over its high back.

My arms are pinned painfully under me, still bound between my legs and attached to the rope around my ankles. I teeter over the edge of the sofa. I try to press my knees against the back of it to balance. Pulling my head up despite the shooting pain, I try to teeter back away from the cushion. I catch glimpses of a dark room, hardwood floor. A light is on somewhere down a hall. I'm shocked. It's a normal looking living room.

His hand is rough on my back, but he keeps me from falling forward. He stands behind me and I scream when I hear his zipper. He rips off my thong and I don't have a chance to try to move or kick. I don't stop screaming when he enters me, slamming his hips against my ass, pushing the sofa. But I hear his grunts and moans anyway. I feel the tearing at my pussy lips.

I try to scream louder.

## 9 Him

"So what was so special about that Friday that you came over to see Lucy when you knew your brother wouldn't be here, Jake?" Killaney isn't going to let this go.

Jake sighs but manages to only give a hint of apology in his look to me. He turns his eyes to Killaney again, "I wanted to check on Lucy. See how she was doing." Here he tries to sound a little stronger, but it comes across as defensive, "She's family after all."

"That's nice. Family *is* important." *I'm not going to be able to hold my temper much longer with this sarcastic fuck.*

Dad moves to stand so Killaney would have to turn his head to see him, but I have a clear view of his warning look to me.

Killaney doesn't stop staring at Jake. "But you were so specific." He looks at his notes, like he needs to refresh his memory of what was said only moments ago. "What was so special about picking Lucy up? You and Max right? Was that the night before or earlier in the week?"

Jake clenches his jaw, but I answer. I've had enough. I'm calm when I say, "It was Wednesday night." Everyone looks at me with a warning to shut up, except Killaney. He's leaning in. "That was the night I punished Lucy for letting another man touch her while she was out with her friends."

I know this is foolish. I shouldn't give this information to the police, they'll only keep me on a suspect list longer. But the more information I can provide, the more questions we can get through quickly…*it'll all come out anyway. I don't care what the police think of me. I only care about finding Lucy.*

Killaney is again shocked at my admission. "So…you punished her *how* exactly?"

"I spanked her with a belt."

He leans back. But he has a quick mind, he recovers from his shock and zip lines down another cable of questioning. "And you knew this? That's why you were worried about Lucy?" He's turned to Jake again.

"Yes." Jake shrugs. "Well…I didn't know exactly what happened that night between them. Not until I saw Lucy that first Friday morning."

"And how was she then…that Friday?"

He looks apologetically to me. But that just pisses me off more. "Answer his questions, Jake." I use the tone I know he responds to, the same one everyone does. The same tone I respond to when Dad still uses it on me.

Jake lowers his head though before answering, "She was hurt." Killaney questions with his hand moving sarcastically in a circular motion on his wrist. "She could hardly walk without wincing. She couldn't sit."

I think back to that day. *Lucy had a hard time sitting even a week later*. My fists clench again. *But she never mentioned my brother visiting. Neither of them did!*

"Did you see any bruises on her?"

"No." *I know this is true. At least that time. Everything would've been covered.*

"Did she tell you that she was injured? Did you offer to take her to a doctor?"

I interrupt, to keep this moving along. It's the lawyer in me. "Detective Killaney. Let me just clarify something for you. My wife never saw a doctor from any punishment I gave her. She didn't need one. She never filed any complaints with the police either. You're welcome to check both of those things. I will clear any forms you may need to speak freely with her doctors."

Killaney reminds me of Lucy. He has such expressive facial features.

*God, Lucy,* where *are you?*

## 10 Her

He finally stops pounding me against the sofa. *He must've come. I don't know. I don't want to know. Oh God...* I start to cry, but this is abruptly turned to a yelp when he tips me down towards the floor and I crash against the hardwood, hard on my back, my head snaps and cracks against the floor. I see stars, but don't pass out again. The ceiling is murky, my vision tunnels for a moment. I roll slowly to my right side. I'm looking through the legs of the sofa at a coffee table, at a brick fireplace opposite.

I hear him walk away. I hear a drawer opened, a metal against metal sound. *A loud clanging of silverware*? I hear his footsteps return to stand behind me. Instinctively, I keep my eyes averted, on the floor in front of me.

He squats down and breathes heavily over me. "You are a nice piece of ass, bitch." A shiny metal huge knife appears in his hand in front of my face. *Oh God, this is it. I'm sorry, Max. I love you! It'll be over soon, baby...*

He puts the knife to the rope between my hands and ankles and I grunt a sigh as my body is given some freedom. I steal one quick glance up as he moves away. *Blue eyes*? Dark hair, stubble. Dark pants, dark shiny shoes. That's it.

## 11 Him

"So assuming that checks out…that Lucy didn't seek the help of a doctor or the police. That still leaves you, Jake. You saw her and you continued to see her weekly for the last several months…" Killaney keeps eyeing between Jake and me.

"Yes." Jake is still reluctant in his answers, but he keeps his eyes on Killaney.

"Because you were worried about her?"

"Because I wanted her to know that she could talk to me."

I have to close my eyes to get the color red to clear. *I don't care if this is my brother saying it…another man, seeing my wife on a regular basis, behind my back*! I want to scream and rampage. Instead, I breathe in and out and finally, unclench my fists. *That won't help find her. I need to stay calm, to help her.*

"And what did she talk about to you?"

Jake shrugs. "Everything. Nothing."

"About her marriage?"

"Sometimes."

Killaney shoots a look of warning at me and glances at Jeff, still standing close by.

"So…were you screwing her?"

Jake doesn't hesitate in answering, "No."

"But you wanted to…?"

And Jake hesitates. *He fucking hesitates.* I push back my chair and tower over him, my fists at my sides. Jeff grabs my shoulder and tries to yank me back. I pull out of his grip and turn towards the terrace, "I need some air." Jake just sat there. Not moving.

*My own brother wanted to fuck my wife?!* Everything is colored red.

## 12 Her

He comes back and nudges my head with his socked foot. *At least it doesn't stink*. I'm almost hysterical again with this thought, but his words cut into the ether.

"You don't remember me do you?"

*I know him*? "I…I haven't seen your face." My head hurts with the effort to speak.

He laughs. "Dumb bitch." But he sounds amused, not angry anymore. "You think that matters to me?" I only shrink in response. He picks me up by my waist again and hauls me to the other side of the sofa, next to the coffee table before dropping me again. I manage to stop my head from bouncing this time.

He sits behind me, putting his feet on me like I'm his ottoman. I start to cry and shake.

"Stop that. Or I'll give you something to cry about."

His voice isn't as commanding as Max's, but the effect is the same. I stop.

He turns the TV on and I close my eye.

It's all I can do to block out the pain, the fear, to ignore the truth. *I'm in a nightmare and I'll never see Max again.*

## 13 Him

I stand just by the terrace doors; the cold spring air cools the heat of my face. The other cops moved away, I don't care where. Jeff comes to stand next to me. *My watchdog.*

I can still hear Killaney and Jake though.

Jake didn't answer him, so Killaney backtracks. "So. Yesterday. Lucy answered the door. You said she was happy to see you. What did you talk about then?"

"She was nervous about her doctor's appointment. But hopeful."

Hearing him talk about how Lucy was feeling, what she was thinking… *Fuck. This can't be happening. None of this is real. It's a fucking nightmare.*

"So she wanted a kid?"

"Yes."

"And she thought she was pregnant?"

"Maybe."

"Was it your idea to keep your meetings secret or hers?"

"I…we didn't really *decide* to keep anything a secret."

"But your coming here. Her talking to you. It *was* a secret…"

"I guess. Sure."

"So what other secrets did Lucy share with you?"

## 14 Her

I wake when he grabs my waist again. I'm a rag doll lifted in the air by a giant child. He walks with me under one arm, against his hip. I watch the hardwood turn to tile and a bright light goes on above.

This time I'm ready to be dropped, but I still fall hard and crack my elbow on the floor. I feel warm blood smear under my right elbow and knee as I move to try to sit up. His foot shoves me back down.

"Stay down, cunt."

I watch as his feet move around the cabinets in the kitchen, but his back is to me. He has dark, almost black hair, straight and short. And he's tall. *Strong*.

He opens a slow cooker and the smell of cooked meat makes my mouth water. I'm hungry. *I'm beaten, tied, raped. And hungry. What insanity is the human body?*

I watch as he puts something on a plate and brings it to where I am on the floor. Through my hair, I get a good look at his face. *Blue eyes, yes. Slightly crooked nose. Needs a shave. Where do I know you from?*

"You throw this up and I won't feed you again for three days." But he rubs my head.

The gentleness of his touch only adds to the stab in my empty stomach at his words. *Oh God. Three days. He means that he will keep me here.*

My mind goes blank. Instinctively, I say quietly, "Thank you." He only laughs and tells me to sit up. He walks over to the counter where he has his plate and watches me.

I'm awkward moving with my wrists and ankles tied. My head swoons. *Go slow, baby.* I finally manage to get to my elbows on my side, ignoring the pain, but I can't sit up anymore. I pull the plate under my chin and take a small piece with my fingers. It tastes as good as it smelled. I eat everything.

But I almost throw up again when he picks up the plate and says, "Good girl."

*Or was that Max in my head?* I fall back to the floor.

**15** Him

I turn to see Jake's face as he answers the question. "Lucy didn't have any secrets."

"Just you." It's a good thing I'm not standing near the sarcastic fucker.

Jake's jaw clenches. Dad steps in between them. "I think you have the answers to your questions here, Detective."

Killaney turns to me and nods back to the table. *No. He's not done. Not yet.*

I walk slowly by the table into my kitchen and return with the glass of scotch. I put this quietly on the table before sitting back down, away from everyone, but I see how Killaney licks his lips. I give him a crooked smile and slowly lift the glass to my own lips, taking a deep drink. I just as slowly lower the glass back down. *I may not be able to punch him, but I can torture the drunk.*

"We know that Lucy's phone and credit cards were left with her purse. You said," he nods to me, "that Lucy would've had some cash, but not much on her. For cabs. We didn't find any money." He pauses to let this sink in. *At least I'm finally getting some information.* "We've set up your phone here to record and track calls in case there is a ransom demand or contact." I knew Dad had rushed this through.

"We should know more later today about fingerprints and anything we found from here." He moves his hand in the air to indicate the apartment. "In the meantime, I need you, Max, to think of anyone who might have wanted to hurt you or your wife. Any employees, former or current. Any cases you've handled. Anyone at all." I nod.

He doesn't move to get up though. "And I *am* going to check with your wife's doctors, friends, and family. We'll keep checking local hospitals; no one with Lucy's description has been reported so far." I lower my shoulders at this news. I didn't realize how tensely I was waiting to hear this. "The news will get ahold of this story pretty quick. We'll want to get ahead of that. A media liaison from the Missing Persons Unit will contact you later today." I nod again. I assumed this. *The zoo will be open for business.*

My voice sounds far away, "Has anyone reported seeing Lucy on the street…near where we found her phone?" The pathetic weakness in my own voice angers me. I want to throttle someone, something.

Killaney only blinks at me. "We're still checking."

*And I know the son of a bitch is lying to me! He thinks I'm a suspect, so he'll keep as much as he can from me for as long as he can.*

I hear the house phone ring and freeze.

## 16 Her

He returns with the big knife. I watch it shine as he moves. I'm not as afraid this time. He cuts the rope around my ankles. I only stretch one leg out, experimenting with movement again.

He grabs my arm and yanks me to my feet. I have rag doll legs. I almost slip back down, but he has a firm hold on my arms. His fingers cut into me. This close, I see he has a mass of chest hair, dark, curly, sweaty. I raise my one open eye to him.

*I know you? ...How? From where?*

He laughs at me. Yanking me around and dragging me down the dark hall.

We pass rooms to the end. I'm still shocked to see the normalcy. There's bad art on walls, stains on rugs, popcorn ceilings. My prison looks just like the house I grew up in, small and normal.

I shake in his grip, but manage not to cry, manage not to trip.

## 17 Him

"You need to answer that. Stay calm." Killaney follows me to the kitchen phone.

I'm disappointed when I see 'P Shannon Cell' on the callerid. "It's Lucy's dad." He nods, but he doesn't move away. *I'm still under observation, I guess.*

I clench my jaw and turn away from him as I answer. "Hello."

"Max! Any news, have you heard anything yet?"

"No, Paul. The police are just finishing up here." I can hear a lot of background noise on his end, a warbled announcement. "You made it to the airport?" My dad took care of getting them on a redeye here.

"Yeah. We should get in early this morning."

"Good. Just grab a cab for here. I think Dad has you booked at a hotel nearby." Dad nods from the doorway. I'm a robot, running on automatic, saying and doing what I need to, but not comprehending anything right now. "Yeah. We'll get it straightened out when you're here."

"PJ's picking us up. We'll get there as soon as we can." I start to say good-bye, but Lucy's mom gets on the phone.

"Do the police have any idea where Lucy could be, Max?"

"Not yet, Liz. They're doing everything though. I have to go. Safe flight." *I can't break down. Not yet.*

## 18 Her

He pushes me into a dark room and I stumble on carpet, my bound hands out in front of me. My knuckles bang hard into something wood, "Shit!" It takes me a second to open my eye against the pain.

"Bet you don't talk like that with your *husband* around?" *What did he say*?

He turns on a low light. I can just see what I hit. It's a wood footboard to a tall bed. I swallow hard. Instinctively, *and with Max's voice in my head,* I mumble, "I'm sorry."

He smiles and laughs, oddly making his face harder. I shake more. "No. I like a filthy mouth on my bitch." I shake my head. "Why don't you try this? Ask me real nice to fuck you again. I know you liked it the first time."

I shake my head. My whole body shakes, my head's just along for the ride.

He takes one quick step towards me and I almost fall over backwards on the footboard trying to get away. My feet scramble, only my tip-toes touch the carpet, the board painfully arches my back. He grabs a chunk of my hair in his right hand and yanks me forward, but not off the board. There's a flash of a dark grin and white teeth before the explosion of painful fireworks erupts as he slaps the left side of my face hard. I can't even scream the pain takes too long to give me back my air.

He keeps his hand in my hair and pulls me up to face him. "Now. Ask me, whore."

My lips try to form words, but I don't know what they are. He rattles my head and I'm afraid he'll hit me again. *I don't think my eye can take that.* "Pl…Please…fuck...me."

He releases some pressure on my head, but keeps his hand in my hair. "We'll work on that." He drags me over to the side of the bed and lets go of my head. I panic, looking around for something to fight him off.

*Who am I kidding? My hands are tied. And he's strong.*

He laughs. I hate his laugh. It's not sarcastic, not evil. It's a laugh you would hear anywhere. "Oh. You wanna have a fighting chance against me? How about I untie your hands and I'll even give you one best shot, Lucy?" He laughs at how I cower away, shaking. *God, I would love to be a man right now. To knock the shit out of you!* But I only cower.

Then it dawns on me. "You…you know my name?"

His smile twists. "I know a lot about you, Lucy."

I try to stall, to think. *Think, baby.* "Like what?"

"You really don't remember me at all do you?" I only shake my head a little. He sneers, laughing at me, "I'll make you a deal. If you can remember *my* name, I won't fuck you…tonight. I'll even give you three questions to figure it out." He's very amused with himself. I don't believe him, but it's something to hold onto. "What's your first question…Lucy?"

*Think*! "Where…where do I know you from?"

His look melts from dark smile to dark frown. "No…that's cheating! Do it again and the game's over."

"Do…do I know you from," *Think!* "Do I know you from my building?"

"No." He pulls off his tank top and I can see that he's strong everywhere. I look away.

"Do you work with…with my husband?" *I can't say Max's name. Not here. Not after what this man did to me.*

"No. But I'll give you a hint…I have met Max." He pulls off his pants and kicks them away. *He's really enjoying himself.* I only have to glance to see he's excited again.

I panic, searching around the room for a hint. *I don't even know where I am. I know it's wooded and obviously remote. But I have no idea how long I was passed out in the trunk. I haven't heard any cars or other people. No one heard me scream. It's pitch black outside the window. It was daylight when he took me on the street.*

I vaguely remember someone saying my name, turning and feeling dizzy. His arms held me up and walked me to a car. That was it.

"Tick tock. Last question."

"What's the first initial of your first name?" I'm risking that he'll think this is cheating, but my mind is blank on anything else.

He only chuckles. "B." He stands a little taller, putting his thumbs in the band of his underwear. I shrink a little more. "What's my name, Lucy?"

*Oh God. I have no idea*. I say the first thing that comes to my mind. "Bill."

He laughs harder and I almost pee myself. You would think I just told him the funniest story while walking home from a nice date. *No one so evil should have such a nice laugh.*

**19** Him

"I think we're done here for now. I have what I need for ViCAP and OC so far. Flash messages have gone out with your wife listed as Endangered Missing." I'm walking Killaney towards the door. I raise my eyebrows to this. "That means we believe her disappearance may put her physical safety in danger. It puts her to the top of the list of adult missing persons." Killaney glances at my dad. I'm sure his contacts had something to do with fast tracking that too.

"Thank you, Detective."

"You signed the report already?"

"Yes."

"Good." He looks me up and down. "Try to get some sleep. Hopefully, we'll be able to resolve this quickly. Someone will be by later to check on the surveillance equipment."

I close the door behind him.

I don't move for a moment though. The color red is back and I need to breathe before acting.

## 20 Her

He stops laughing abruptly. "Nice try." He pushes off his underwear and I try not look at him at all. He moves to sit on the bed. I have a moment of picturing myself running, but that would be foolish.

I don't know him, but I know myself and I know people. Instinct. *He'd only like it more if I fight or run.*

He pats the bed next to him, "Hop on." I sit quietly, willing my hands to stop shaking. *Nope. They think they should be clawing his eyes out and they won't stop trembling.* I look at the red, raw skin under the rope.

*He seems willing to talk, maybe that's something I can use...*

"Why are you doing this?" I try not to jump when his hand comes up and brushes my hair back. *And why are you being so gentle now? Is this a new game?*

"Because I wanted you the moment I saw you. Actually, before that even. Something in the way your husband talked about you. Something about him. I knew."

I look down. I don't want to talk about Max. I don't want to hear this man talk about him, but something in what he says... *Clues or is he messing with me*? "You knew what?"

With one finger, not gently, he pulls my face up to look into his eyes. I'm trapped in the darkness of the blue. "I knew little Lucy is used to taking orders." He smiles, moving his finger to the left side of my face. I wince at his light touch. I can only imagine what I look like. "And I like a bitch who is already mostly housebroken." He laughs at his own words.

## 21 Him

I stand with my hand on the door for a while. I hear Dad move a little more into the hall towards me, but he stops when I turn around.

I can finally release the anger I've been barely holding back. I move quickly down the hall to pass him, but Dad grabs my arm. His grip was always a vise. His voice is calm, in control, commanding as usual. "You don't want to do this right now." Too many years raised under his belt, his complete power, I don't move. "*I* will talk to Jake."

I want to tell him to fuck off. I thought it plenty of times growing up. But he's the reason I am who I am. He saved our family. *I can't disrespect him no matter what. Even now.*

"Answer me, boy."

"Yes, Sir."

He lets go, and turns quickly to move into the dining area again. I follow behind slowly, still seething with pent up rage.

Jake hasn't moved from his seat. Jeff still stands next to him.

Dad nods to Jeff. "This is a family matter. You can go."

I nod to Jeff when he looks at me before moving. He leaves quietly, but not before telling me to call if I need anything.

Jake finally looks up at Dad. It's the same expression he wore as a kid, whenever Dad had The Look and Jake knew he was in trouble. In the beginning, I tried to protect Jake from our stepdad. That never worked. I would get twice the punishment and Jake would still get his. By the time Ron adopted us officially, we were both toeing his line.

Now I don't look with pity or sympathy on Jake. I want to beat him myself.

"Jake." Dad takes a seat opposite him, hands on the table. "What were you thinking? Seeing your brother's wife like that, in secret?"

*That's not where I would've started.*

Jake shrugs. "I wasn't thinking. It just happened really." *He always tried to get away with the innocent act.*

"That's not an answer, boy."

Jake looks to me, but I only shake my head, fists clenched in my crossed arms.

"I came to see how Lucy was, that first time. I knew how angry Max was with her…for what she did. Hell, *I* was mad at her." He tries to laugh, but stops at the look he gets from Dad. "But I also know what men do in this family when they're angry. I just wanted to make sure she was okay."

"That wasn't your right, Jake." Dad says exactly what I'm thinking this time.

"She *is* family, Dad. I have a right to make sure she's fine…" But he isn't convincing anyone, not even himself. He knew what he did was wrong. *And he did it anyway.*

Dad speaks so quietly that I almost can't hear him, "But you weren't checking on her as a brother would a sister."

Jake swallows before answering. He was never a good liar. He learned a long time ago not to try with Dad. "No, Sir," He looks at me, "But we were just friends. Nothing more. Nothing more than that ever."

Dad nods. I have no choice but to nod too. I know he's speaking the truth. It's what he's *not* saying that has me still clenching my fists though.

*He wanted her.*

"So what else weren't you telling the police?" Dad could always read us. He knows as well as I do that Jake was holding back with Killaney not just about his being here earlier or the night I beat Lucy.

He looks at his hands while he answers, not wanting to see my face I guess. "She was struggling with everything. Lucy…she didn't know if she could live up to what Max demands of her." He looks at me briefly, then back at the table. "I saw her when she got her last period..." He takes another deep breath. Hearing him talk about Lucy, about her so intimately, it takes everything not to shove the table away and choke him with my bare hands. "She was crying. Saying she didn't want to tell Max. She didn't want to disappoint him."

"She told you all that?" Dad is sitting back. I don't think either of us had any idea how close Jake and Lucy had become. We've hung out together plenty. We helped him celebrate buying a new building to make his new architectural offices and home. We've spent holidays together. *But Lucy was confiding in him before me even. And I didn't have a clue about it.*

I remember how sad and frightened Lucy had been the last time she told me her period had started. I held her all night, reassured her with little touches and kisses. The next morning, she said she felt like we were going to be lucky very soon, that she wanted nothing more than to have my child in her arms next year. I was so proud of her for not staying sad, for bouncing back so quickly. *I had no idea that maybe that had more to do with her talking to Jake than me.* I clench my jaw harder at this thought.

"Yes. She also said she wasn't sure how she felt about raising a kid," he glances at both of us now, "the way we were raised."

Dad doesn't say anything for a long time. It takes longer for me to get this simple statement through my head. *Lucy talked to Jake about this?* She never said anything to me. We talked about her fear of miscarrying, not being able to give me a child, but nothing about this. *Of course, she would also know better than to question me.*

*So maybe she was questioning Jake because he was the next best thing? Or was she really afraid of her future with me? Could I have missed that?*

I shake my head. *I can't believe that.* I know Lucy. I know what's in her heart. I know she wanted to make me happy, to please me. But I also know that this is what made her happiest. She might have worried, but she never would have questioned our future. *She had faith in me, in us. I have to have the same faith in her now.*

Dad finally speaks up again, "Do you think she could've run away?" I hadn't even thought this was a possibility until right now.

This weakness is not something I've ever felt. *I am powerless.*

## 22 Her

He pushes me back and I don't resist. "All the fight gone out of you already?"

I shake my head, but I don't resist when he pulls my dress up and puts his hand between my legs. He stops and I squeeze my eyes shut, expecting to be hit again.

Instead he stands and pulls my legs roughly apart to stand between them. He pulls my dress up and yanks it over my head, my arms trapped in it. I can't hardly see through the film of material, but I stay still.

I hear him spit and just make out that it's into his hand. He puts this to my pussy before dropping both his hands to the sides of my head. The bed bounces and his face comes close to mine; the dress is a welcome barrier now. He enters me hard. I'm still raw from before, but I don't cry out. I'm oddly calm. Max's voice keeps telling me I have to *stay calm, think*.

He doesn't take long, grunting into me again, calling me bitch and whore. He makes me say I like it. When he stands, I start to move the dress down, but he growls at me to leave it. I don't know where he is. *Still in the room*? I can't really see between the dress and the low light.

I hear his breathing above me and feel him pressed between my legs again. *Oh, God. Not again. He can't be hard again already.*

I hear the rip before I feel it. The dress is pulled and giving way in front of me. He has the shiny knife again. He pulls my arms away from my chest roughly and cuts the ropes.

Stepping back. "Get that off." I sit up, moving my arms and hands to get the ropes to fall. My skin burns in the air. I don't stand, but push my dress and bra off my shoulders; he'd cut them in half already. I hiss at the belt marks and try to be gentle.

I move my head, so my curls cover most of my chest.

"Lay back down." And I do.

*He's right. I'm a well-trained puppy when it comes to taking orders.* My eyes fill with tears. The left burns.

*I can't believe I'm here. Like this. Naked before this man. Lost. Raped.* I can hardly think the word. I hear Max's voice. Hear him telling me to stay calm, to not cry. To hold on. But my body screams louder. The pain between my legs outshouts anything in my head.

I press my knees together. I shake with unshed tears and unvoiced screams. My hands shake with unyielded anger, with unyielding fear.

*He's hurt me so far. But he obviously intends to keep me…to keep doing this to me. I have to breathe hard to not throw up. I'll be okay. Max will find me. I know he tracks my phone, my calls. He'll know I'm missing long ago. He's already looking for me. Max.* I can't help myself, I shake with silent tears at thinking of him.

*I can't picture him finding me here…like this.* I turn my head and try to hide under my hair, covering myself with my hands as best as I can.

**23** Him

"I…I don't know." Jake shrugs and shakes his head. "Maybe. I don't know where she would've gone though."

*Jake may think that he knows my wife. She may even have confided in him. She's too trusting in people. But I know Lucy.* I square my shoulders. "Lucy wouldn't have left me. She had that choice once. She knows her place is here with me."

I can't see his face, but Dad nods once. Jake just looks down.

*I know my wife. She may have felt that it's okay to talk to Jake since he's my brother. But she would never dare to leave me. She would never dream of stepping out that door without my knowledge. I gave her the choice once to leave or stay. With that first slap, I gave her the only choice she would ever have. And she made it then. She stayed. She does know that she belongs here, with me.*

It's Dad who finally breaks the silence again. "Jake. Not a word to the police about Lucy's fears. That won't help to get her back." He turns to me, "And I think you've given them enough information about how your marriage works. You want them to eliminate you as a suspect and concentrate on who really has her…then you need to swallow your pride."

I nod. He's right.

"Take a shower. I'm going to arrange a car for your mom. She'll want to be here when Lucy's parents get in." He turns to Jake. "Why don't you get some sleep in the guest room for now?"

And we both move to do what he says. No arguments.

## 24 Her

I still my tears, breathing deeply, again listening to Max's voice in my head. I have to turn my head to see what he's doing. He has something metal in his hand when he returns to the bed, but I can't figure out what it is. *A small broken chain?*

"I used this on Bitch when she was small." His eyes twinkle in the light. He's so happy with himself again. *His own biggest fan. He almost looks nice, like someone I'd see...where?*

*I'm too drained to think anymore, Max. Just let me sleep.* And despite my fear, despite my brain racing to figure out what is happening, who he is, where I am...I close my eye. I close off my brain from the pain and fear.

I don't even open it when I feel cold metal on my neck. I don't open it when I feel him shove me further onto the bed or when he puts more rope around my wrists.

I allow myself the one escape I can…I sleep.

**25 Him**

I open the door and Lucy's mom is immediately embracing me. I hug her back and look into my father-in-law's eyes. They look as bloodshot as mine. No one's slept.

Her brother, PJ, brings in their bags and sets them in the hallway. I shake his hand. I haven't seen him since the birth of his son. His wife, Cathy, stayed home with their kids.

I lead them down the hall and into the dining area. Mom has a full spread of food out all ready. She's been buzzing around here getting everything back in order and cleaned. She needs to stay busy to keep from crying more. Dad told her not to in front of me again.

But the moment she hugs Liz, they're both crying. I turn towards the kitchen. I can't stand hearing it. It rips at my own tears, the ones I've kept bottled in the pit of my stomach so far.

I hear Dad warn Mom, "That's enough, Alex."

I get another cup of coffee and walk back in. Mom is sniffling. Liz is burying her face in Paul's chest, but she stopped crying too.

I fill them in with what's happened since they landed. "The tech just left here. They're monitoring all calls and messages to my phones – here, my offices, cell. So far, nothing. But they believe that this might be a ransom demand…" *I'd pay anything to get Lucy back. Then I'd hunt down whoever had her and kill them.* This thought calms me. "No one used her credit cards. They were tossed with her phone and purse. No prints on anything." Dad has been pushing every contact he has to get everything sped up on the investigation."

"So they think she was kidnapped on the street? In broad daylight?" Paul is choking this out. His face is red. *So like my Lucy.*

"Yes. But they're checking for any witnesses still. It's Saturday now, so downtown is pretty quiet. They know the security guard in the lobby of her doctor's building recognized her, but said he doesn't remember seeing her yesterday. And no one from the doctor's office saw her either."

I take a seat on my sofa. Paul moves to sit in a chair opposite me. "So what's next? What can *we* be doing?"

"I'm giving the police my full cooperation. I have a private investigator our firm uses too. He already has all the details. I won't leave anything to chance, Paul." He nods. "For now, the police have asked for a list of anyone who might've wanted to harm Lucy. If you can think of anyone, anything at all that will help…"

Liz laughs sharply, a hysterical sound. "No one would want to hurt Lucy. Everybody loved her."

Paul gets up and puts his arms around his wife again. "We know that, dear. But the police have to start looking somewhere."

Dad speaks up from his spot at the table. "Maybe she should lie down, Paul. Alex has the guest room ready."

Liz only shoots him a hard look. "I don't need to lie down, Ron. I'm not a child!" She turns quickly though and walks down the hall to the bathroom, slamming the door behind herself.

Paul gives an apologetic look and goes to follow her.

PJ looks uncomfortable and takes a seat at the table finally. Mom hands him a plate. She needs to feel useful right now to someone. *I know how she feels*.

Lucy's mom has been struggling with me since our wedding. She still likes me, but she doesn't like that I'm in charge. Really she doesn't like that *she's* no longer in charge of her daughter.

I let Lucy talk to her as much as she wants, except when she's grounded from using the phone. Three days after I beat Lucy that Wednesday night was the first time I had to tell Liz that Lucy couldn't take her call. She yelled and threatened me. I stayed calm, but I eventually had to hang up on her.

When Lucy was able to call her again, I listened while she explained that she was fine with me punishing her like this. I was very proud of Lucy that day. She stuck up for us to her mom. We've had a neutral truce since then.

Thinking about Lucy, remembering her voice, her smile, her, I feel even calmer. *She* can't be lost to me. I will find her. She belongs to me, with me. I have to keep faith in that.

I'm jolted out of my thoughts by the phone. Everyone looks to me. Liz and Paul quickly come back into the room as I answer the call. It's only the lobby downstairs. Killaney's back.

## 26 Her

I wake with one thought. *Max doesn't snore.*

I lift my head and two pains fight for dominance, the left side of my head and my neck. My head wins, I stop moving. I swallow, but something metal pokes at my throat.

I slowly open my eye. My left still won't budge. Light is just starting to come through the window. I try to lift my hands to my throat, but this burns my wrists more.

I'm tied again. I slowly move my head, not lifting it. I can see him next to me. Snoring. In bed.

*Don't think about that. I was raped! He raped me, Max. How am I supposed to not think about that?*

*I'm losing it.* I need to breathe. Whatever's on my neck makes it difficult to get deep breaths, but I calm down. I close my eye for a moment. *Breathe.*

I open my eye again and see that he has two ropes in his hand. One I can see leads to my wrists. The other trails across me body, up to my neck. *A collar. I have a collar on? Oh God.*

*Don't panic!* I obey Max's sharp tone. I always do. I swallow rapidly several times despite the strain on my throat.

I slowly move my wrists towards him. *Who is he, Lucy?* I shake my head slightly. I don't know. I gently pull the ropes from his loose fingers. *Don't wake him.* He doesn't move, more snores.

I have the rope ends in my hand. I almost laugh, giddy with freedom. I feel lightheaded for a moment.

I slowly. Oh so slowly. Move my legs towards the edge of the bed. I want to jump up. I want to run. But I go slow, just like Max is telling me to do. My head shakes with Max's commanding voice.

I stop. I can't see him anymore; I've turned away, but I can still hear him snoring. *Good.*

Another inch. My left toes are on the floor and I push my upper body gently up with my burning wrists. My head swoons.

But it's the low growl that makes my stomach leap.

I look down and a foot away. I can just make out what looks like a pile of black clothes on the dark carpet. But the pile is growling. And I can see white teeth. A lot of white teeth stare back at me.

He stirs behind me and I'm trapped between him and this beast. I'm yanked back onto his body by his hand in my hair.

"Morning." His smile is full of the same white teeth. Too many of them. I hear a high scream. *Mine*. I strangle it, shaking, too afraid to give him anything, even my scream.

He laughs. "I see you met my other bitch." At this the dog jumps up on the bed. I don't turn my head.

I can smell the same hair I choked down yesterday. I can smell its breath. I can hear its panting.

He pets the dog and me at the same time. The shine of the dog's teeth is inches from me. Her ears are back and she still growls low while licking his hand.

I cower against him for protection, keeping his arm between my face and the beast. He laughs and continues petting me the same way. *I'd like to bite his hand; I'd like to have her teeth for weapons*.

## 27 Him

Killaney introduces me to the media liaison, Eve. She's young, pretty, with a face you'd want to see on TV. She smiles a lot at me and puts her hand on my arm like we know each other already. I move away to sit on the sofa again. Killaney introduces himself to everybody else, taking names down on his notes.

Liz doesn't wait for Killaney to finish writing, "What can you tell us? Have you found anything that will help?" Her voice is unnaturally high and Paul squeezes her arms. She pushes off him though and walks closer to the detective. I can see Paul's patient and frustrated response. *He's never been in control in his marriage.*

"No, Ma'am. We're still looking, though. We have a canine unit now on the street and we're canvassing the area around where her purse was found." He gently pats her arm and says slowly, "We're doing everything we can."

She only nods and takes the seat next to PJ at the table.

Killaney turns back to me. Dad walks to stand next to him. "So, Max. Do you have that list for us?"

I hand him a piece of paper. It's not long, a few employees I've had to fire recently, a disgruntled client or two, a few more defendants, no one I can think of who would do something like this though. He glances at it. "We'll go through these today. Anyone else…anyone who might have been jealous of you or your wife? Of your money?" He looks around the apartment. It's not opulent, but I obviously have money. "Anyone who would be jealous of your fame?" I'm not famous, but I'm well known in certain social circles. It's the price of being involved with popular bars and restaurants. Everyone asks for favors. *But no one would do this.*

"No." I put my hands to the sides of my head, shaking no. I've given this same list to my investigator.

"Any ex-girlfriends or boyfriends on here?"

"No." I clench my jaw thinking about Lucy's ex-boyfriends. There weren't many, but I have my investigator looking into any in the area too.

Killaney turns to Jake. He's been staying out of my sight, standing near the wall of windows. "Anyone you can think of?"

Liz looks surprised that Killaney would ask my brother this. *So, she didn't know about their friendship either…Lucy really kept it a secret from everyone.* I look at my brother. His face is neutral again.

"No. I…I don't think anyone who ever met Lucy would want to hurt her." Jake doesn't meet my glare.

Liz nods and starts to cry into a napkin. Mom turns to walk out the room with a nod from Dad.

Killaney gestures to Eve and she moves to stand in front of me. "I'd like to get you ready for an announcement for the press, Max." I know they've been mobbing downstairs. "We'll keep it short, no questions." I nod at her.

She appraises me. "This message is very important, Max. This could be what brings your wife home." I nod again and don't shake off her hand on my shoulder. I've always hated when women get too familiar too quickly. *She's probably easy to get in bed too.*

"What am I supposed to say?" I know what I want to say. *I want to promise whoever has my Lucy that I'll kill them when I find them.*

"We'll run the photos and details we have before and after your announcement. But I'd like you to hold this one up." She hands me a glossy enlarged image of Lucy. It's one I took on our honeymoon. She's smiling and a breeze has her curls floating on the air. Rome is blurred in the background. I remember her laughter with that picture.

Seeing her smile now, I have to stop from crying by clenching my fist against my leg. *I can't lose it.*

"You'll need to say that she's been missing since yesterday. That…" She pauses and looks at Killaney who nods at her, "That she may be pregnant and in need of medical care. Say a few things about her, what you love about her. The more you can say to make her real for anyone watching, the better." Her voice is annoying. It's too friendly, too happy, too fake concerned and trying for consoling.

She waits until I nod to continue, "This part is very important, Max." I look up at her. She smiles at me again. *I want to hit her. To knock the smile off her face. I want to hit something anyway*. I smile back. "You need to stay calm on camera if you can. Tears are fine. But no anger." *I could choke her*. I only nod once more.

"We'll go downstairs to meet the press in ten minutes. Why don't you wash up a little? No shaving though…it'll look better on camera." She turns to where Liz and Paul are sitting. She doesn't see the clenching of my jaw or the shaking of my fist on my leg. "And I think we'll have her parents stand just to your side." Liz frowns angrily at the appraising look Eve gives her. "But you won't say anything…not this time anyway."

I groan thinking that there will be more of this, being on camera. Begging someone to give me my wife back. Begging someone to call with information. *Begging*.

Dad squeezes my shoulder. The barely hidden anger on his face echoes my own.

## 28 Her

"Get down, Bitch." And for a second, I'm confused if he means me, but he doesn't let go of my head.

The large black dog gets off the bed immediately. *Well-trained too, huh?*

I try to stay calm as his hand moves from my hair to my neck, just below the collar. He twists my head around to his. I can see his hard on. I press my legs together again. I'm still hurting from yesterday. I fight back the tears.

"I…I need the bathroom…please?" He grins at this. He likes being in control. My mind runs from this thought. I always liked Max in control. *I can't compare being here, under this man's control now.* I stop anymore thoughts of Max.

He gets up, but keeps his hand squeezing the back of my neck, pulling me with him. He pushes me towards a door and shoves me in, turning on the light. I stand facing him, trying to hide behind my hair.

I look at my bound wrists. My skin is broken in spots, dried blood colors the rope. "Can you untie me?" I hate how tiny my voice sounds, like I'm asking for a new toy. He responds to it with a grunt and grabs my wrists.

He's rough untying the rope and I have to stop myself from wincing out loud, only little hisses escape my lips. He keeps grinning at me. He takes the rope to the collar out of my hand.

With my hands free, I turn a little and see a toilet. "Can I have some privacy?"

"Nope." *I didn't think so, but it was worth a try.*

I've gotten used to doing this in front of Max. He doesn't let me close doors to him, but the humiliation of this man watching me as I stumble a little and take a seat is almost worse than the pain shooting out from all over my body. My head, eye, throat, arms, wrists, back, legs, pussy. The ride in the trunk, being thrown around here, being beat with his belt. I hide my tears under my hair. When I finally pee, I wince. He was very rough and it's just another spot that hurts. I wipe carefully.

He tugs on the rope a little and I wince louder from the pain on my throat. Tiny pinheads push all around my neck. I get up and he moves to stand next to me.

I look away, despite this pulling on the collar more. I hear him pee and grunt. And fart. I gag against the collar. He laughs.

I can see myself in the mirror, just my shoulders and head, but I gasp. I don't recognize myself. My left eye is swollen shut. The lids are two angry red and blue puffy half circles meeting where my eye should be. The skin around it is a deep red and purple mix spreading onto my cheek and forehead. My right eye looks oddly small in comparison, an island of pale skin and blue water. The bruise spreads to this island even.

The collar on my neck shines in the light. It's a metal choke collar for a small dog. The tiny prongs pinch into my skin. My shoulders and neck are crisscrossed with belt marks. These I'm familiar with, but never above my butt. *Max would never have hit me like this.*

I don't take comfort in this thought. I run from all thoughts of Max. I yell at his voice in my head to shut up. *Shut up! You're not here and you can't do anything about any of this!*

I can feel all the parts of my body that are broken and sore. *I'm battered.* That's the word. I've heard it on TV. I've seen images from movies. I've seen my own body hurt, punished. *But not like this.*

*I think the only spot not hurt is a baby toe.* I almost laugh at this. *You're getting hysterical again, baby. Yep. I know, Max. I'm going to die laughing…*

I close my eye and clutch the small vanity, shaking and choking on my tears. *No. I won't give this man my tears. I won't as long as I can help it.* I make a promise to myself to hold back as much as I can. He can beat me and take what he wants from me physically…but I can withhold my tears. I'm strong enough for that. *That's my girl.*

I take a deep breath in. And it's familiar. My eye pops open and I see why and see him standing behind me. He's without any expression, just watching me.

He tugs the rope and I move to follow him out of the bathroom.

He stops at the bed. The black dog is inches from my legs, still showing teeth. He sits on the bed and orders me to kneel. I obey, but move to be away from the dog some more.

I know what he wants before he puts his hand to the back of my head and pushes me down towards his swelling dick. Despite the pain, I resist, "Wait." He lets me lift my head again. "What if…What if I can guess your name right…will you…does your deal still stand?"

He laughs. I have to stop the windows flying open in my head, letting all the sanity out, at hearing his laughter again. It's too normal, too sane to belong to this, to him. I take one shaky breath in and out before meeting his eyes again. "Sure. Why not." Instinct. He's arrogant, full of himself, and he actually wants me to know who is.

And I know his name now. *But do I save this get out of jail free card for later or use it now?*

The thought of him fucking me again turns my stomach and I know I don't have the courage to wait.

## 29 Him

It's drizzling out. Everyone's crowded under the awning of my building. Eve assures me that the address of the building won't show on TV. The press knows where I live, but that doesn't mean I want every rubber-necked freak out there to know, the ones who can't turn away from an accident on the side of the road. They always slow down to watch.

It's cold, but I left my jacket upstairs. Liz huddles next to Paul to my right side. I look at Lucy's smiling face in my hands. *I'll find you, baby*.

Eve gives me a nod, all the lights and cameras and microphones are aimed at me. I hold up the picture.

I say what Eve told me to say. I talk about Lucy. I choke on the words "pregnant" and "medical care" but I get it out. "Lucy is a sweet girl. She's never hurt anyone. She should be home with me now. Please."

I have to swallow several times before I can continue in a stronger voice, my usual commanding voice. "Please, if you have any information about Lucy's disappearance. Call the hotline." I pause. This is all I'm supposed to say. The cameras start to dip even. "Lucy. Baby. If you see this. Know that I'm *going* to find you. I'll have you back where you *belong* soon, baby."

The reporters start shooting questions at me. I ignore them.

I turn and walk back into my building before anyone can stop me. I don't want to hear Eve talk more about the hotline or Lucy.

## 30 Her

I read once that the brain is an amazing computer. Capable of processing all sorts of valuable information in the blink of an eye. The greatest mysteries are locked deep inside us, as memories. The key to unlocking them can be as simple as a hint in the air.

I blink my one good eye. I don't want him to think I tricked him, if I have any hope of him keeping his deal. *It's only a small hope anyway...but it's all I have.*

"It's not Bill."

"Is that your first question?" His laugh is still in his voice. I can see that he's still hard too. I look away. I look down. *Concentrate.*

"No." I swallow. "I'm just going over what I *do* know about you all ready."

He laughs. I clench my jaw, but this causes my left eye to hurt, so I stop. I need to focus. "Take your time. I got all day." *Arrogant asshole*. I haven't cursed this much, even to myself in months. I feel numb with thinking this. *Focus!*

"You met my husband before you met me." He nods. He's enjoying feeling superior. He drops the rope and leans back on his palms. I keep my eyes focused up to his to avoid looking forward, to avoid seeing his dick.

"This obviously isn't the city." He nods again. "So we didn't meet near my home." He nods slowly, licking his lips.

"Did I meet you while on vacation?"

He grins. "Yes."

I know the answer all ready. "In Wisconsin?"

He chuckles, "No."

"Where are we?"

His look darkens. "That's cheating and your last question." It was a risk. I was hoping he was so full of himself that he'd give me this information, that he would think it wouldn't matter. *But he's not that dumb*.

"We met in Rome." I say this with a stab of pain at the memory. I was happy in Rome, with Max. Our honeymoon was a time when everything seemed good and possible. I was confident in my place with Max, in his love for me.

He smiles, it spreads across his features. It's a genuine, bright smile, a nice smile. I'm thrown off balance and sit back on my heels. His face is almost movie star pretty, softer.

"What's my name, Lucy?"

"Ben." This is the man I met briefly in the hotel bar with Max. I slapped his hand when he touched my leg. He has the same candle. The one the hotel gave as a gift. My bathroom at home smells just like his…just like the hotel's.

The brain's a crazy computer. It can hold onto the smallest details for so long. That was over six months ago. *But I remembered his name.*

## 31 Him

Upstairs, I head into our bedroom and quietly close the door. I need a minute away from everyone's eyes. I can hear their hushed words. Everyone is asking Eve how she thought the press meeting went, if she thinks it will help, how soon we should do another one with Lucy's parents this time…it goes on.

I walk into our closet. I like it in here. I leave the light off and breathe. Lucy's smell is here. Her sweet, orange blossom scent clings to her robe, to some of her clothes, sweaters. I turn and close the closet door to be surrounded by her. The leather belt on the back of the door swings against my hand. It's where it always is unless I'm using it on her.

This makes me think about Jake again. *How could she keep a secret from me? That she feared how I would raise our child?* I hold my head in the dark and fight the tears. *I* can't *believe that.*

Lucy feared me; she feared my anger. Sure. I even told her once that I *wanted* her to fear me, that it would help her to not mess up, to not break my rules.

*But it was more than that*. I liked that she feared me. I liked seeing it in her eyes every now and then.

And I know that she liked it too. *She did. She told me she did.* In the dark, after a spanking. She would tell me that she liked how we were, that she loved me. I would hold her, and she always said she felt so safe and secure. Especially after a punishment.

*I know my girl*. Lucy didn't know her submissive side when I met her. I saw it in her. I recognized the signs, saw what she could be for me. I didn't go slow. I didn't have patience. I didn't ease her into anything.

I broke her and made her mine quickly. I forced her to submit to me completely. I gave her only one choice, one chance to back away from her destiny with me. I smile thinking about that night. She was so scared. And so yielding.

She always is when she sees my anger. She always knows just what I need. Her.

*She can't be lost. I need her. Here with me.*

*I can't believe anything else. I have to hold onto two things.*

*I will find her.*

*And when I do…I'll straighten out this mess of keeping secrets.*

## 32 Her

He claps his hands and I jump at the loud noise in front of my face. "So you figured it out finally?"

I nod. "You've been stalking me all this time?"

He chuckles. "Don't flatter yourself." He sits up and walks to an open closet. I watch from the floor; I can't move with his dog right next to me. He comes back wearing sweatpants and a t-shirt. He throws a sweatshirt at me and I quickly put this on, grateful to be covered.

*He's going to keep his promise, his end of the deal*? I almost laugh and cry with relief, but keep myself in check.

"I didn't stalk you; I checked you out. It was easy to get info on your husband. I saw a few online posts with your pictures at events over the months." He picks up the rope and tugs me to stand.

We walk with him leading and the dog trailing behind me into the kitchen. I can feel Bitch's breath on my legs.

He nods to the stove and I take this as direction. Plus, I'm hungry. He drops the rope and gives me free range around the kitchen to make us food. He's gone for only a second to open the door for the dog. Not long enough to do anything, but I do take note of several large knives on a stand near the stove.

I have to roll the sleeves of the sweatshirt up, but I'm glad that it's so big. It falls to just above my knees.

He talks while I make us scrambled eggs and toast. I have to hold back tears remembering this with Max. Our mornings together, how I loved cooking for him.

He keeps a close eye on me whenever I'm near the stove. "I won the money for that trip. I've never won anything before, but hit the jackpot on an Indian res near here. I promised myself that I'd take a trip of a lifetime with it. I guess I got the jackpot again right here." He laughs and slaps my ass hard. I try to move away from him a little.

"I found out your address and went there a couple of times, to see how easy it would be to get in. Figured I would be spotted if I tried it there." He laughs and reaches for the rope giving it one hard tug, causing me to choke and cough. "Better not burn my eggs, bitch!" Still coughing I move the pan off the flame. "I thought your husband kept you on a shorter leash than this." He's still laughing.

"I even came back and waited one whole week for you to come out of that building once. When you finally did, you had that driver right there waiting for you. I gave up, figured I would never get near you again."

In the beginning, Max didn't allow me out much. Especially after I messed up that night with Rich. I shake my head thinking about this. *Better to not think about anything but right here, right now, baby.*

I hold both plates and follow him into the living room. He makes me sit at his feet and eat off the coffee table. He sits on the end of the rope. Between bites, he continues. *He certainly does love to talk... or at least hear his own voice. But I need to know this... it might help.* "And then. Yesterday. My lucky day again." He laughs at the frown I give in return to this. "I told myself that I was going to try one more time. I deserved another chance. And I had business near the city, so it worked out. And there you were, all by your lonesome."

He takes my unfinished breakfast away from me, and makes me crawl with him over to the door, opening it for the dog. I watch as he puts the plate on the floor and lets the dog eat my food.

He walks me back on my hands and knees to sit in front of him again. "I couldn't believe how lucky I was though. I got there just in time to see your husband leave. I wasn't even sure you were in there, but I didn't have long to wait. It was easy to follow your cab downtown. Even easier to nab you right off the street." He snaps his fingers in front of my face. "Just like that."

He laughs watching me try not to cry. "Oh, go ahead...have a good cry, girl. I don't mind." He yanks on the rope and I choke again, crying a yelp out loud. The dog comes over and snarls at me. "Down, Bitch." *Me or the dog*? Bitch heels, but keeps an eye on me. "The hardest part was finding a deserted spot off the Skyway to move you to the trunk and tie you up." He laughs a little.

*He said skyway...that means we're in Indiana*? And I remember something else about him... *He said he was from Michigan*. I glance out the window at the woods still spindly, without leaves or buds. *This could be Michigan*. I keep my eyes down to hide how I feel. It's not much, but I know sort of where I am at least. And it's not far.

*Max...please, find me. Please hurry!*

## 33 Him

"You have to eat something…" Mom is pushing my plate back towards me. It's leftover roast from yesterday.

"Eat what your mom's made for you, son." I lift my eyes to Dad. He has The Look going. I've been living off of coffee and scotch for four days, only taking a few bites of all the food Mom has made for everyone. I know what I look like. I'm numb from bad dreams, little sleep, little food, little control. But I still respond to him. I still do as I'm told. I pick up my fork and don't taste what I chew.

Mom kisses my head and walks towards the guest room. They've stayed with me. Liz and Paul are in a hotel on the next block. We've all been holed up here in this apartment each day, waiting for any news, giving the press what they need to keep the story in the headlines, hopeful for any information. *Nothing. Fucking nothing.* No fingerprints, no calls, no demands for money, no leads on where she could be. My investigator, the police, no one has any fucking news.

I've avoided work, obligations. Dad's taken care of what he can from here. Friends have been by, but I've even avoided that. I can't deal with friendly right now. I can't deal with forced niceness, or repeating the inexplicably small amount of information I know.

Screaming. Hitting. Raging. That's really what I want. *What I need right now.*

I pick up my plate and go to the kitchen with it. Mom has the house all in order, but each day I hear her crying softly, behind closed doors. Just like when I was a kid. *Is that what Lucy does? Waits till I'm gone for the day and cries to herself?* I try to imagine that.

I know I hurt her. There were times when I allowed my anger to really show. If she talked back for the second time in a week or forgot how I like something to be done a little too soon after I'd reminded her, I'd hurt her a little more than usual. I'd leave her with tears streaking her pretty face. I'd be rougher in bed with her. I'd slap her around more.

I always showed Lucy my love and forgiveness afterwards, too. I always cradled her in my arms, soothed her tears away. I let her know that she was my good girl again, that she had all my love, no matter how many times I would have to tell her a rule or show her how to please me.

And she always responded the same, with more tears at first, begging my forgiveness, apologizing for whatever she did wrong. Sometimes it would take longer to soothe her, to get her to calm down and realize that I wasn't mad at her anymore. She always thanked me for punishing her, just like I taught her.

I can't imagine her crying the next day again. *Maybe from pain...that one time...* I know she cried from pain days afterwards. I would come home for lunch and see that she'd been crying. But she needed a reminder that lasted. She belongs to me. If she was in pain longer, it was because she deserved to be punished longer, to be reminded of that each day. She never said anything, never complained about the pain.

*She didn't say anything about Jake coming over either though.* I frown at this thought.

*No. She was only needier.* She needed my constant touch and affection. She was always this way after a punishment, but especially after a harsh one. She'd need to see a smile on my face after any little thing she did to please me. She'd get through most of her chores before I was even home for lunch, trying to show me her willingness to do exactly as I demand. I always made sure to be more attentive and loving to her, to give her the reassurance I knew she needed.

I remember Mom crying when she and Ron were first married. Jake doesn't remember any of it. I would sneak towards their bedroom door and listen as he'd punish her, for every little thing. He didn't give an inch. We all did exactly as we were told or faced his punishment. And Mom was the same as Lucy. She'd run around trying to be on her best behavior for Ron. Like a puppy needing a treat, she'd follow him around the house. And he was always so loving to her. He'd light up when he came home; she'd light up whenever he smiled at her.

Ron's discipline gave my life stability. It saved us. Jake and me. From Mom. Saved her from herself.

I give this same stability to Lucy. She knows what I expect, exactly what is expected of her. She knows what it takes to please me, her complete obedience.

But I don't kid myself. *I need more than Lucy's obedience.*

My dreams have been filled with punishing her, for not being here. My anger has nowhere to go. In my dreams, I give myself the release I need. I beat her, more than I ever have in reality. I use my belt, my fists. I hit her with the buckle. I watch her bleed under my hands. I choke her until her eyes are popping.

I wake from these dreams sweating, crying. Hard.

I wake myself before I come. The monster in me, in my dreams, takes her every time, takes her bleeding body, her beaten, broken body, takes what's mine to take.

In my dreams, Lucy submits to whatever I do to her. She takes whatever I give. She's the same as she is in real life. My obedient, submissive, sweet wife, her screams fill my heart. She gives them to me freely.

I don't kid myself. *I am a monster.*

*My Lucy is God knows where…and in my dreams, I torture her.*

But every waking hour is torture for me. This complete feeling of uselessness, helplessness…I've never been powerless before. I've always known what to do to get something done. I've never let anything stand in my way.

*But this...I have no choice.* I have to let others take the lead. I have to sit back and wait. And there's been nothing. No good news so far. No helpful information. Just more waiting.

I fill my dreams with the anger I can't let out in the daylight. I have to hold it together for everyone watching.

I smile for a minute, indulging in a daydream. I picture Lucy here now, her little hand touching my cheek. She would know how to calm me. She would know how to reassure me.

*I hope wherever you are, baby, you're picturing me too. That you're holding on...staying strong. Picture my arms around you, protecting you.*

I can't let myself think of any alternative...*I will find her.*

## 34 Her

*I hate you, Bitch.* I've always been a dog person; but from this point forward, I don't know that I'll ever look at one the same.

She lies next to me, a large, stinky black rug. But she's free to move around. I'm locked in her cage. She's locked out of it.

With my hands tied again, in a ball, I take up the same space she does probably on the dog bed. It smells like piss and hair and everything evil. I turn my face away, but it doesn't matter. I smell like it now, I'm sure.

She sniffed at me the first hour, trying to figure out why I'm in here and she's out there. Her big wet black nose ran all along the metal bars.

Ben went to work. He called in sick for two days. *He's sick all right.* I don't know what he does. I don't care. I just hope that he's gone for a long time. This is as close to peace as I've had in days.

Every inch of me is hurt. He's gone from almost nice, civilized even, letting me sit at the table, wear a smelly shirt to crazed maniac, hitting with his fists and feet, not caring where his blows land. It always ends the same. I squeeze my legs together. I'm sore and swollen, throbbing. My pussy lips are torn, my thighs bruised, my ass…I can't think of any of this. I close my eyes again and breathe. Small, shallow breaths to avoid the smell. I'm used to the collar now; I don't even feel it as I breathe.

Before he left, Ben carried me in here and laughed when he said that Bitch would keep me company today. He means that even if I somehow got my hands loose, it wouldn't matter because his dog would treat me like a chew toy if I tried to leave.

He demonstrated this very effectively last night. Slurring and drunk, he sat back on the sofa and made me walk towards the door. Inches from my freedom, hand on the doorknob, Bitch growled a low deep rumbling of hunger right behind me. Ben told me not to move until the dog was back at his side. *You couldn't have paid me to move*! My legs were liquid with fear.

I open my eyes again and watch her. She's just itching to get her teeth into me, I know it. Her black eyes have stared at me all day. *I know what you're thinking…that I took him from you. Well, you can have him!* I say this out loud. I think I'm going crazy. She only tweaks her ears at my voice. She rolls over and closes her eyes again.

I've heard Max's voice more today. He keeps pressuring me to figure a way out. Like I'm not trying.

I have several barriers. Dog. Man. Cold. Clothes. Pain. Hunger. Weakness…I am weak with everything. *How many days has it been?*

*But you can't give up, baby.*

*I'm not. But…I can admit… No. I can't!*

I need to just stay calm and wait. I'll be found. Max will find me. I have to have faith in that.

*But what if he doesn't…*

*You better get that thought out of your head, little girl.*

*Max. I pretend the hair stuck to me is yours. The nasty dog smell is yours after a hard run. The pain between my legs, yours. All my pain. Yours.*

But I don't fool myself for long. There's metal around my throat. Metal under me poking through the thin bed. I am not home. I am not safe.

*And yes. Dammit. I can say it…I blame you, Max…you said you'd keep me safe. There.*

*Ben…*you *talked to him, Max.* You *made* me *talk to him.* I think back…how I flaunted my submissiveness on our honeymoon. *How proud you were…you liked how other men saw you, saw me.* I felt so free. It was the first time I truly embraced what I was. *Max's property.*

I didn't say those words to myself; I didn't have to. He'd said them. He's said them plenty since then. But that was the beginning of me accepting it. *No. The beginning of me wanting it that way*. And I was proud of myself for showing off for him.

I moan, a soft low cry.

I've held my tears in for as long as I could…thinking of Max, how we were, how I was…I let go and cry, big open sobs of snotty release. Bitch stirs, but only to move her head a little away from me.

*I was free…and now I'm in a cage with a fucking dog and I can't get out! So stop talking to me!*

But I stop crying at this thought. *I'm sorry, Max. I'm sorry.*

*I need to stay calm. Focus. Not go crazy.*

*Maybe not go crazy should be first on that list…*

## 35 Him

"The police haven't found anything?"

"No." Laura shakes her head pityingly at me, and looks around the room. Lucy's mom and dad are talking in hushed tones by the terrace doors with PJ. Mom is quiet at the table; Liz had her crying again after watching a piece on Lucy's disappearance on the evening news. Dad and Jake are next to her. "They just left. The eye witnesses that may have seen Lucy Friday weren't very helpful. Too many conflicting stories and details to be of any use. My investigators aren't giving up, but… We don't really have anything to go on right now." My voice breaks with admitting this out loud. I wipe my hand over my face to cover my need to yell.

"I'm so sorry, Max." Laura's eyes fill with tears. She's called every day, but I told her to stay away while the mob was still downstairs. A week after Lucy's disappearance and no new news, the press is onto some scandal or something. There's only a few reporters and cameras downstairs now.

I pat her hand on my knee. She's Lucy's best friend and a sweet girl, but any sign of tears or softness puts me on edge right now. Her expression changes though and she leans in a little. I frown. "I…I just wanted to let you know…" She's whispering this to me. "Tracy talked to the police this morning. When they came to the office…"

I knew this was happening. Killaney told me that he talked to Lucy's doctors yesterday. He seemed only a little more convinced that I shouldn't be his main suspect. I assumed they'd already talked to her former boss and co-workers. My investigators had. I only nod.

"She…she told them that she thought *you* might have something to do with…" I only nod again. I'm not surprised. Not even angry. "I'm so sorry, Max…" I pat her hand again. No use even thinking about any of that.

Tracy can say what she wants. I don't care. As long as it doesn't interfere with the police investigation.

I'm getting used to being numb. Scotch helps.

Laura gets up and walks over to Liz, Paul, and PJ. I stay on the sofa with my head in my hands. Dad comes over to sit next to me, but he doesn't say anything. He knows there's nothing to say.

I need some time alone. A week surrounded by people. A week of being investigated myself. *A week of losing my fucking mind with fear and hopelessness.* I get up and walk into the bedroom, quietly closing the door. I haven't shed any tears, except the ones in my dreams. I have to hold it together, until Lucy's home. But I can feel the tears are close, my eyes burn with them. My gut is retching.

I calmly walk into the closet and punch the wall. The impact feels good. I can breathe again. I shake my hand and go to the bathroom to rinse it under cool water. The knuckles are red, but I didn't break the skin. This has been my routine lately. The only release I allow myself.

The man looking at me from the mirror isn't me. His eyes are hollow, deep in dark circles, jaw covered in the start of a beard, hair matted down from hours of running my hands through the waves. And I stink. Too much scotch, too little bathing.

My hands have been idle for too long. I need to do something.

I go back to the closet and get my running shoes. I have to get my head clear again. I have to get myself under control again. I won't last if I keep this up.

*Fuck. I have no idea how long I'll have to last…Nightmares usually end when your eyes open. This one just keeps going.*

## 36 Her

I slept. I lost track of time. Bitch didn't. She gets up and leaves the back room, to wait for him. I can see the light is gone from the window.

I shudder. *No, please... a little longer.*

His boots come into view and I hear the metal scraping as Ben opens the door. I yell as he drags me out by my hair and arm.

All wind is knocked out of me when his boot meets with my stomach. A fiery pain, a thudding pain, a new pain. I can't breathe. My eyes try to gulp in air, my left still barely able to open. My mouth is a fish seeking bubbles. My body wants to stretch, to get the most air, but my brain takes over, I ball up.

He picks me up before I can stop gasping and carries me to his bedroom, tossing me on the bed. I almost bounce off but he's on me too quickly.

His dick shoves into me from the side. He uses my whole body to push and pull me onto himself. His grunts have the stale smell of liquor. I can feel my lips tearing again. I shudder at the wetness. My body has taken over, providing what my brain refuses. I've been wet for him when he rapes me. It's a small relief against the pain. *Or is it the pain that gives me relief?* I run from this thought.

I can feel him. I've tried to back away, to shrink from all knowledge of what he's doing, to hide in oblivion of denial. But there's no denying the feel. The pain. The push. The pull.

I laugh, hiding this in a cry out. He doesn't go as deep as Max. He's not as big. In a crazy moment, I have to bite my tongue to stop from yelling this at him. *Don't be stupid, baby. Hang on.*

But I pray for a time when I can shout this at him. When I can tell him that I laughed while he fucked me.

I break down in tears, because he doesn't stop. Ben just keeps pushing and pulling, fucking me harder and grunting.

He staggers back when he's done. I take one big gulp of air, but this is turned to screams when he brings his fists down on me, my head, arms, back, legs, side. He tries to turn me over, but I hold onto the mattress through the cover, my fingers are claws. He's too drunk, stumbling with his punches. I protect my stomach, my face.

Finally, he stops, panting. I can hear his belt jingle as he steps out of his pants.

I shake and cry, sobbing into the mattress. Everywhere hurts. But I put my bound hands to my stomach. *Please, no. Please.*

"Get up." He pushes my hips on the bed.

I obey. For fear of more fists, I move quickly. I don't know how, but I stand next to him. He grabs the rope holding my wrists and leads me into the bathroom. He turns the hot water on and shoves me towards the shower. With my hands bound, I turn the knob to cooler before stepping in. He doesn't notice. He's drunk.

"You stink, bitch." *You stink, asshole*! But I'm grateful for the warm water. I put my hands forward, the ropes are wet and my sores hurt more. He laughs. "No. You'll stay tied tonight, cunt!" He watches as I quickly wash. I'm stiff and can't move easily, but I'm thankful to remove any trace of him or his dog. I'm yanked out before I can rinse all the soap off.

He dries me roughly. I try not to look when his hand and towel goes between my legs. There's blood. Naked and still dripping from my hair, he leads me towards the kitchen. "Make me something to eat, bitch." He slurs.

*Does he come home drunk every night? He's been drinking every night so far…Can I use this?*

But he opens the door and the damn dog is at my heels again.

*How am I supposed to get out of here, Max?*

## 37 Him

"Did he have any ideas where Lucy would go?" I hear Liz's voice bouncing high in my living room. She sounds a little angry and a whole lot hysterical. I walk in, closing the door quietly behind me, wiping sweat from my eyes.

I hear Killaney's voice answer her in his calming tone, "No, Ma'am."

The run did what I needed it to. I'm clearer. I was able to think again without feeling the need to either heave or hit. I walk down my hall slowly.

Paul is sitting behind Liz. PJ stands next to her. Mom, Dad, and Jake all stand separate to the side. Liz is inches from Killaney. She looks and sounds upset. I have a tightening in my stomach, but I keep walking.

Liz's eyes dart to me. She's all anger now. "What did you do to her?!" She takes one step towards me, but Paul stands and grabs her arm, PJ moves closer to her too. "What did you do to Lucy?"

Everyone moves in a little. I stay where I'm at. I address Killaney calmly, "Do you have any news? Any new leads?" I fear what he's going to say.

He steps in front of Liz a little. "No. But we did have an interesting conversation today with a former co-worker of your wife."

I relax a little. I was expecting this. On my run, I went through how this would play out. What would be the best and fastest way to get the police off this trail and back onto the one that leads to finding Lucy. I know Tracy squawking about me will cause waves. I just have to wait it out.

Jake and Dad are both giving me warning looks. I know Dad doesn't want me to go into my marriage more with this detective; he thinks it'll look bad for me. *I don't care about that. I care about finding my wife.*

"We spoke with Rich Tesson."

I can feel my jaw clenching, but I keep my hands loose. I don't like hearing that name. I only narrow my eyes, waiting for the rest.

Killaney pretends to look at his notes. "He said he was good friends with your wife until you stepped in." I still remain silent. "Said he was afraid for her. That you had a violent temper." Silence. I can hear Liz breathing heavily behind him. "He even said you threatened him. To break his arms if he so much as looked at your wife again."

Killaney isn't going to continue. He waits out my silence now. "Yes."

Killaney's surprised look. "I'm going to need more than that, Max…"

"Yes. I told Lucy that she wasn't to see or speak with him again. And I told him the same."

"Did you threaten him?"

"No. I *promised* him." I can't help the little grin I let slip. It's a small release of the anger I feel at the memory of threatening the fuck who dared to touch my wife.

"And did you threaten Lucy…?"

"No." I take a breath and exhale it with a sigh. I can see Dad's small head shake. Jake's too. "I didn't need to threaten my wife, Detective. We've been through this already. I gave Lucy an order and she obeyed it. No questions."

"You sonofabitch!" Liz pulls against her held arm. Killaney turns a little so she can see me. But he keeps his eyes on me; he's waiting to see my reaction, but I give none. "Did you hurt her? Did you hurt my baby?!"

Killaney raises his eyebrows. He wants an answer to her question.

Dad moves to step next to me, but I give him a small shake of my head and stern look to stop.

I look at Killaney as I answer. "We've already been through this. I punished Lucy for letting Rich touch her."

"Oh my God." Liz is shaking, staring at me in disbelief. I ignore her.

"That was the night you spoke of spanking your wife?" I nod. He turns towards Jake. "The same night you were worried about Lucy and started seeing her on a regular basis?" Jake nods slightly. "And this was about five months ago?" He's back to looking at me. I can see that he's trying to stay calm, for Liz's sake I'm guessing. I'm already calm.

"Yes."

Killaney purses his lips and stares at his notes. Liz doesn't like his silence. She pulls free from Paul and faces him again. "Aren't you going to do something? Arrest him? He just admitted to *hurting* my daughter!"

He speaks slowly and calmly, turning to her a little more, "Ma'am…we are looking into every possibility. But…" He looks at me again and I know he'd like nothing more than to arrest me. *He'd like this to be over.* "But I can't arrest him for this."

"Why not?" She glares at me, "Look at him. All smug. He just confessed to you."

He shakes his head. "Mr. Tesson didn't file charges. And neither did your daughter. I have nothing to go on, Ma'am."

I speak up, ignoring Liz, "You spoke to Lucy's doctors, too. They had nothing to report, did they?" Killaney shakes his head. He's not convinced. But he's stuck. "So where are you on the investigation, Detective? What are you doing right *now* to find my wife?"

He shakes his head again and looks at Liz as he answers. "We're doing everything we can. Right now the hotlines are our best chance of finding something that will lead us in the right direction."

She shakes more and collapses into herself. Paul leads her to sit on the sofa while she covers her face and cries.

Killaney moves towards the front door, but stops close to me. "I'm not through with this line of questioning…" When I don't move, he finally walks out.

I turn to head into my bedroom, but Liz jumps up to confront me. "You hurt Lucy? You *spanked* her?"

Paul has ahold of her shoulders. I look at him. He's not shocked by what he's heard tonight. Lucy didn't tell him everything, but just before the wedding he talked to her. She admitted to how things are between us and said she was happy. I look back at Liz. "Yes."

She shakes and almost spits in a hysterical, angry laugh, "I can't believe this. I cannot believe you are standing here…saying this!"

"Liz." I take a deep breath. With the frustration of the last week, of having everyone here, of living in a fishbowl of questions with no answers, of being powerless to help my Lucy…I have to take a moment to get my anger in check. "My marriage to your daughter is not yours to question."

"The Hell it isn't!"

"Paul." I ignore Liz. "I'll see you both in the morning." I turn back to my bedroom door, but Liz isn't shutting up.

"No. You'll answer me! What did you to Lucy? Have you done something to her...do you know where she is?"

I don't turn all the way around, just enough so I can look directly at Liz again. "Lucy is mine. My wife. My property. What I've done to her is none of your business." She only blinks at me, in a state of shock. I don't soften my voice or expression, "But I can assure you that this..." I shake my head. "...I want Lucy here. Now. Where she belongs. I had nothing to do with her disappearance."

I don't wait for her response. I quietly close my bedroom door and head to the bathroom. I'm shaking. My anger and pain is too close to the surface. I ignore the yelling in the living room.

Dad and Mom, Liz and Paul, the quieter voices of PJ and Jake, I head into the shower to drown them all out.

## 38 Her

*I'm on TV again. Well, my picture is anyway.* Ben likes to watch the evening news before bed. He likes to snore through it. The copious amounts of whatever he's been drinking finally took its toll. I finally have my few moments of peace.

He keeps me on the floor, forcing my head against his knee. Bitch gets to be on the sofa with him. *Better her than me.*

The news has been running Max's pleas. Mom and Dad have appeared a few times. Ron and Alex. Jake. PJ and Cathy. I've even seen a few interviews with friends. A crying Laura. An angry Tracy. Former co-workers. Neighbors. I never knew how many people thought they were close to me. People I barely know have shown their faces with tears for the cameras.

Mom and Alex looked terrible, crazed in the eyes with too much crying and not enough sleep. I've avoided looking at myself in the mirror. Too many bruises and cuts, not enough food or sleep. I'm wearing down. I can feel it. I can feel my mind chasing down a hole, any light getting less and less. I can still hear Max, but it's painful now, too distant to be real. I can only pretend to be strong for so long.

On TV, Max promised to find me. To get me home. Where I belong.

He said it in that voice I know so well. I responded. Despite sitting at this man's feet, bruised and beaten, with every inch of me covered in pain, I respond each time. The news loves to show that part of his plea, the epitome of the distraught husband, barely holding back tears. *But I know the truth. Max was barely holding back anger.*

Each time, it brings the usual stomach zing, pussy flutter. I let one little tear fall the first time I heard it.

When Ben is fucking me, I've tried to think of Max. I've tried to pretend, to make it through. Sometimes this helps. Sometimes I can almost forget all the pains and hide in a memory of being with Max, feeling only the pain he gave me, feeling only the love of his strong touch. I stop these thoughts now. I don't have the energy to keep up the image for long.

I put my hand over my stomach. The news is reporting on my possible pregnancy again. I don't know if I am. I could be.

Tired. Sore breasts. Nauseous.

*But then again... I've been tied, raped, beaten... that's bound to make a girl feel a little badly, right?* I hold back my laughter.

When Ben heard that I might be pregnant…I can barely hold back my shudder at remembering….

Ben had grabbed me by the arm and punched my stomach. Hard. And laughed. He was delighted with his own threat, "You'll do exactly as I say, bitch, or so help me, I'll punch you again and not stop until you're bleeding out of your cunt one way or another." *He can really be quite poetic in his crazy rants.*

He believes that this gives him more power over me. It does.

But he was nicer after that. Well…a little gentler anyway…he lets me wear the sweatshirt more and unties me when he's home. He's still brutal. I bleed from my head to my toes. I'm a bruised, bloody pulp. Even my baby toe is sore now. I choke a sob or laughter. Can't tell which.

*Oh, God. He'll be home all day tomorrow. It's Saturday. Today, it's been a week.*

I don't know how much longer I can hold myself together.

*And if I am pregnant…* I cradle my stomach. I can't think about that.

*Hold on, baby. I'm trying…but I need something to hold on to, Max.*

I let my tears fall silently. Ben still snores, but I feel Bitch stir above me. I think she's smarter than him. She alerts him to my mood changes. I sniffle and wipe my nose on the sweatshirt. The crusted blood from this morning wipes off and I have to stifle a small cry.

Bitch sits up, making Ben move and curse. I close my eyes for the one more second of peace I'll have. I almost don't scream when Ben grabs my hair and yanks my head up towards his lap. I swear Bitch is laughing at me, her ugly teeth exposed, watching me have to suck her master's dick.

I imagine biting the head off. I imagine her biting my head off. I try to hide inside my head…

**39** Him

I wake to the phone ringing. It rang all night. It's a reporter again. No comment. I hang up.

At least Lucy's pictures are splashed all over the news again.

The interviews with Tracy and Rich put the story back in the limelight. The poor husband turns out to be abusive asshole and possible chief suspect. Not news, exactly, but it does make for good TV.

The phone rings again. It's Killaney this time. He starts speaking the moment I pick up. "We have a lead. A dark blue sedan that was seen near where your wife went missing." He's out of breath. "I'm at your building now. I'll be up in a minute." He hangs up.

I dress quickly and knock on the guest room door on my way to the hall.

Dad comes out to living room as I open the door to a red-faced Killaney, "We have a description of the car, no plates yet, but we know it's Michigan. A Florida couple saw a woman that could've been Lucy being led to it. They're from Michigan originally, so they remembered that much."

He's starting to believe me, starting to believe that I have what he calls a "freak" relationship with Lucy, but that I didn't have anything to do with her being taken or missing. Liz isn't convinced. She refuses to come back here, just waits in the hotel for Paul to give her news.

"So…?"

"I need you to let us take the lead on this, Max. Your investigator needs to back off and give us the room we need to see this information through."

I agree. But I'm lying. He knows it too. *I won't let anything stop me from doing what I can to find Lucy.*

"The car description matches the one seen in your neighborhood last month. A delivery guy complained about it blocking the alley for three days, so he remembered it. But he can't confirm the license plate was Michigan. He only *thinks* it could've been." That information came from my investigator a few days ago.

"This is good news." Dad claps my shoulder. Any news is good right now, but this is far from a strong lead.

I have to hold onto something, though, and this is the best we've had so far.

*Hold on, little girl. I will find you!*

## 40 Her

I wake to Ben fucking me with his usual grunts, groans, grinding.

I close my eyes, but this pisses him off. He grabs my throat, "Open your eyes, bitch." I do.

"Tell me how you want it."

*Oh God. Not more of this crap.* "I want it hard." He slaps me. My left eye is a mess of broken blood vessels and spidering rivers of bruises. The bone feels twice the size still. I yelp. He balls his hand into a fist and I squeeze my eyes shut, trying to pull my head back into the bed.

"You wanna try again, bitch?"

I know what he wants. "I…want you…to fuck me harder…" He puts his hand back on my throat. "I need you…need your big dick…in my wet cunt." *His second favorite word.* "Please…harder…" I'm getting good at acting in his one-man show. I even throw my head back like I could be coming any minute, but I'm really just trying to get his hand off my throat. "Make my cunt…make me come…" *Oh God.* I get a wave of nausea and dizziness. His hand is cutting off my air. "Please…" He finally comes, but takes his time releasing my throat, laying on top of me, crushing my lungs.

When he finally moves, I roll away, coughing and retching. He kicks my ass and I fly off the bed. I land hard on Bitch, who yelps and whines. I roll off but not before she gets my arm with a good scrape of her teeth. I scream and scramble away like a crab. He laughs and calls Bitch up to the bed, but she doesn't move for a minute. I stay on the floor, clutching my bleeding arm. Bitch finally stands, but doesn't jump up. *Good! I hurt her too.*

Ben gets out of bed and kicks me hard on my thigh, his toenails cut into me. Bitch follows him, limping out the door.

I get up slowly. My back creaks, stiff, but I can walk. I think he may have damaged a rib when he hit me last time. The pain was intense and I can feel it throbbing again, a white hot pain that shouts above all my other spots crying out. I move slow, taking in shallow breaths and panting every few steps.

He already removed everything from the bathroom that could be helpful. The tiny window above the shower isn't big enough to get through. The windows on all the rooms don't open, painted shut years ago, nailed securely yesterday by him. I'm trapped and he's confident that I won't be getting loose.

He intends to keep me here for a long time. Ben showed me yesterday the "fun toys" he was buying online to use on me. I shudder thinking about the whips, straps, masks, shackles…I can't breathe and think of these things. I stop. *Breathe.*

I hiss as I wash my arm in the sink and wrap a towel around it. The teeth marks burn and throb. *Hell, my whole body throbs.* I stare at my reflection for a second.

I have fist marks, belt marks, hot metal spatula marks, cut marks. Every inch of me is covered. There's blood in my hair from my right ear. My right wrist is purple and swollen. My upper lip is cracked and scabbed. My left eye is swelling again. *I'm a mess.*

*And I'm trapped.*

I can't get out of here. I can only wait and hope.

*But I'm losing hope, Max. I'm going insane losing hope. I can't deal with what he has planned…*

*I'm going to have to do something. I can't stay here. He'll kill me eventually. In a drunken rage, he'll do it without thinking.* I start to cry again, but shout at myself to stop.

I can't afford to let go. I have to think. I have to stay alert. *Maybe I can find something that will hurt him. Maybe while he sleeps…*

*But what about Bitch?*

I drop my head in desperate blackness. I can't fight them both off. I can't even fight at all.

I look at myself in the mirror again…I'm only getting more broken by the day…mentally and physically. I try to stand up, to take a deep breath. But I wince at my reflection. *Be strong.*

I hear Ben shouting at me and I turn away from the girl in the mirror…*I can't be her today. I can't be strong when I'm this weak.*

**41 Him**

We're gathered again. Liz even came, but is staying near the door, away from me.

Killaney is debating with Eve about the release of the lead. It seems without any of the license plate numbers, there's a chance that giving this detail to the public could be more harmful than good right now.

"If we throw this out there, then every crack pot in the tristate area is going to be calling with information on a dark blue car. It could take us weeks to get anything out of the hotline that could be of real use."

"Yes…but we need to keep the story going. Right now we're seeing a good response to the…" Eve glances apologetically at me, "the negative publicity Max is getting. But the story won't stay front and center if we don't feed the reporters something new quick."

I break in, "Could giving this information lead…" I don't want to say it, "Could whoever has Lucy panic, thinking we're close to finding her?"

Killaney nods. "Then we're not releasing anything." I turn to Liz and she nods, meeting my eyes for the first time. "But I agree, Eve. That we need to keep the press dangling. We'll all give new statements this afternoon. And up the reward again."

*If the press wants drama, I'll give it to 'em.*

## 42 Her

I watch the news, waiting to see Max again. I hope I'll get to see his face one more time before Ben drags me to bed. So far there's been nothing.

Ben snores. Bitch snores. His hand is in my hair on his knee as usual. Bitch is next to him as usual. He's drunk as usual. I tuck my legs under the sweatshirt more. I'm cold and afraid to move too much. Last night when I tried to get more comfortable on the floor, he smashed my head into the coffee table for waking him.

I turn my eyes to the TV. I can just hear Max above the snores.

"My wife has been missing since last Friday." He looks tired, like he hasn't eaten or slept. I want to touch the screen. My eyes cloud with tears but I blink them away. Max is giving all the details again. Nothing new. *You have no idea where I am, do you?*

The reporters ask questions this time though. "How do you respond to the allegations that you were abusing your wife?" "Did you have anything to do with Lucy's disappearance, Max?" "What about the ex-boyfriend…Do you think he helped her get away?"

I don't know who they're talking about. Ben laughed yesterday, saying the police were looking at Max as their chief suspect. He didn't tell me why. He was his usual smug, drunk, and brutal, just with the added pain of his all-too-normal sounding laughter.

"I didn't abuse my wife. Sure, I spanked Lucy when she needed it…" He shrugs and even smiles for the camera. The reporters go crazy asking all sorts of personal questions. I'm shocked watching him talk about me, our marriage so casually. *I'm missing and he's acting like…like a macho ass! Like it's no big deal to air the details of our marriage on the news! Like he's proud to claim himself a dominant husband and me his submissive obedient wife.* It's just like the crap that made Ben notice me in the first place.

Max winks at the camera. It's the look he gives me when he's happiest with me. The smile, the love, the wink, I always know I've pleased him when I see this. I'm confused and frustrated. *What the hell?!*

Bitch stirs and farts. Ben takes his hand out of my hair and waves it in front of his face, lazily, slurring, "Fuck, Bitch! Let her out!"

I get up cautiously, watching man and dog. Bitch slides off the sofa. She's still limping. She whimpered when he made her get up on the sofa earlier. She's hardly moved all day. I smile at this, showing her my teeth.

She eyes me, but doesn't growl. She's a little warier of me now. *Good.* I let her lead the way to the door. I slowly reach for the knob. There's no growl. I open it quietly and let her out.

My heart is racing. This is as close to the door as I've been by myself.

*What...what can I do?* I'm almost hyperventilating with the shallow breaths I have to take.

I still myself and turn to see if Ben is watching me. His head is back on the sofa and I can hear his snores again. He's been drinking since breakfast.

I take several breaths in and out. *Calm, baby. Focus.*

**43 Him**

"I think that should keep your story in the headline for a while." Eve looks pleased. *She's a parasite*. She acts sweet and concerned, but she only cares about the TV cameras. She talked in the elevator non-stop about how she's just waiting for her big chance.

I concentrated on what I wanted to say. I warned her already that I was planning to throw myself on the fire, to make myself sound like an asshole, to flaunt my dominance, my marriage. I don't care. I just need to keep Lucy's pictures and the reward and the hotline on TV, blogs, everywhere. I'll do whatever it takes. *If that means that every person watching thinks I'm the biggest asshole around, I don't care. I just need Lucy safe and back with me.*

Eve was of course thrilled with the idea. Killaney not so much. Dad definitely not.

It was Liz who had the final word though before I closed the door. I told her and Paul to give a statement about me tomorrow morning, something along the lines of what Liz has been thinking of me the past few days. "You really love Lucy, don't you?"

I only nodded. I didn't trust myself to not breakdown. And that wouldn't work if I was supposed to convince the vultures downstairs to keep feasting on our story a little longer.

## 44 Her

*This is foolish! I can't get away. I don't even know where I am.*

*But I have to try. This is my shot. I know it.*

*Options?*

*Can't go out with Bitch outside.*

*Knives are hidden. Don't know where.* Ben's removed anything I could use against him. I glance at the fireplace tools. He even took the poker away.

I don't think hitting him over the head with anything would do much. *He's so drunk it'd probably only wake him up.*

I can't make it to the kitchen and back for the keys without him hearing me; he has too many. *It's like a damn jingle bell.*

I look down at my bare feet. I'm naked under this sweatshirt. I'm sore all over. I can hardly breathe fully. But my adrenaline is pumping. I feel my heartbeat going crazy.

I look again at Ben. He snores. I breathe in as deeply as I can and shake and stretch my arms and legs as best as I can without making a sound. I need to warm up.

*It's dark out, cloudy. Bitch is injured…Ben's drunk…*

If I can get a head start…I've been training. Running almost every day for months…

I barely hear the scraping of Bitch's claws on the wood steps outside.

I slowly open the door and let her walk in.

Quickly. Quietly. Turn. And close the door behind me. And I freeze for one second.

*I'm outside!*

*RUN!*

I run.

**45 Him**

Jake opens the door for me. He stayed out of the debate about my message, but the look on his face tells me everything. He's glad. And he's afraid for me.

Allowing the story to shift to me is a risk. The police, my investigators…they'll keep searching, tracking down this car. And Killaney assured me that the hotline will still generate new leads, even if the reporters make it sound like I'm the reason for Lucy's disappearance. "People don't care about the why. They'll call in with any detail just to be a part of something bigger. A headline story."

*I hope he's right.*

Jake hands me a coffee. I'm off scotch. I need to be focused. I've been running every day again. Just later at night to avoid the press hanging around downstairs.

"How are you holding up?" We haven't talked much, more through other people, talking around each other.

I still don't want to talk to him. I only nod and walk towards my bedroom again. I close the door on Eve calling her local station contacts.

**46** Her

I run and don't look back. I don't feel the gravel, the dirt, the twigs. I make for the woods. I run.

I don't feel the branches hitting my legs, my face. I don't feel my ribs crying against the exertion. I run.

I hear Bitch bark. I zigzag in the woods, stopping to see the door open and Ben stagger out. I suck in big gulps of cold air.

Ben's holding his head and yelling, "You better get your ass back here, bitch." He's still drunk, having a hard time standing. He and Bitch limp out the door and down the stairs.

Instinct. I wait.

*RUN!*

I wait. Bitch is more injured than I thought. She's not listening to his command to chase me down. She's staying by his side, sniffing.

Instinct. I run full speed towards the street, making a lot of noise when I get closer to it.

Instinct. I stop.

*RUN!*

I wait. I stay hidden, crouched in the dark. Ben and Bitch stumble after me. I can hear them, but hardly see their shapes against the weak light.

I quietly creep back in the direction I just ran. Towards the house. *It's my only shot.*

I stop. Ben is still heading towards the street. He's screaming and yelling, stumbling. I don't see him as much as hear him. But I don't think Bitch is with him anymore. I don't hear her bark. Or sniffing.

*RUN!*

I run. As fast as my feet can go. I run. I apply every bit of focus I've learned over the months of training.

I run. Arms pumping. Legs pumping. Feet barely touching the ground. Heel. Toe. Air. I run.

I think I can hear Bitch behind me. I don't look. I don't turn. I run.

I make it up the stairs without feeling her teeth. I make it through the door without feeling her teeth. I make it into the kitchen without feeling her teeth. I grab the keys off the counter without feeling her teeth.

And then I hear her low growl. It's the same one I heard that first night.

*She's tasted my blood. She won't stop chewing.*

Instinct.

I grab the iron skillet and turn in one swing.

Crack.

*Right across her snarling fucking teeth.* Bitch goes flying and I stumble back into a cabinet.

I recover, scrambling with my arms to propel myself around the corner. She's still shaking her head, trying to get up. I still have the keys, and I run. I think I saw blood and teeth on the floor as I jumped over them. I don't stop. I run.

I'm out the door and down the stairs in one jump. Skidding across the gravel, bouncing back up.

*Focus.*

The car is parked where it was when he first brought me here.

I see Ben, a shadow figure against the lighter gravel, too near. And he sees me. He starts jogging towards me.

I grab the door. Locked. *Fuck*!

I fumble with the keys. Pressing every button. The trunk opens; the doors release.

I get in. *Lock the doors.*

*Start.*

I reverse. Fast. Gravel spins under wheels.

I scream when I hit him. The impact slams me forward, head hitting the top of the steering wheel. The trunk slams closed.

I look, but don't see him. *Where is he?*

*Go, Baby!*

The car bounces and loses traction. The car jolts and settles. *His body under the wheels?*

*Go!*

I don't stop. I careen out to the street, almost going into a ditch, before correcting and driving.

I keep looking in the mirror. I don't know if I expect to see him chasing me. I drive.

I'm down the road and I'm still looking for him.

I start to shake.

*No. I can't. Not yet. I have to get away. I have to get safe.*

I touch my left cheek. I press hard enough to cause tears. But it does the job. I can focus again. I drive.

## 47 Him

I only come back out when most everyone is gone. *I've had enough of the zoo for today*.

Mom immediately puts a plate of food in front of me. I give her a small smile. I've been eating more. I know I need my strength. I'm focused again. I don't taste anything. I don't care what I eat, but I go through the motions.

I smile though, seeing what's she made, chicken parmigiana. Lucy's been taking cooking classes. This is one of the things she actually makes better than Mom now. I don't say anything, but I like the little reminder of Lucy.

I keep trying to picture her here for a little while each day. Most days I only get a minute or two that I can concentrate, only a moment when I can almost hear her voice in the other room. I can almost see her sleeping in our bed.

I can picture her now leaning over me, the smell of her hair, the feel of her skin as she'd brush against me. I can hear the smile in her voice as she'd ask if I like it. I can almost reach out and kiss her neck.

Dad sits next to me, interrupting my thoughts of Lucy. "How are you holding up, Max?" I clench my jaw. *Tired of that question.* I only nod, taking another bite of food.

"I had a talk with Jake today..."

He knows I don't want to talk to my brother, or hear about him. I clench my jaw again, putting my fork down. I don't make eye contact.

"He asked me about your mom. Not about how she's doing through all this," I look up. Something in his voice. *He's trying for tender. Not really his strength.* "More about how she was when we first got married. When I adopted you boys." I don't say anything, so he continues. "I think he's trying to make sense of what Lucy was going through. To think through if she might have, well, left on her own..."

We've been through this. The Florida couple reported that Lucy could've been hugging a man and leaning into him, walking along the street like a nice couple in love. I don't believe that.

I shake my head, but I don't interrupt him. I wouldn't dare to interrupt Dad. "Jake doesn't remember much of those early years. He seems to have forgotten all about that tiny apartment you lived in. Well, he was so young..."

His eyes travel around my place. "I know he thinks I was harsh on you...on all of you." His voice takes on a little of the edge I'm used to. "He doesn't remember how much discipline your mom needed in the beginning. How wild she was, lost. I loved Alex the moment I saw her in that coffee shop. I saw her sweetness buried under her hard life. I saw what she *could* become. Having you boys in my life...well, that's just been...more than I ever thought I'd get in this world."

He's never spoken to me like this, this warmly. He's been encouraging, supporting, giving before. But not warm, not really. It makes me a little uncomfortable. I don't know how to respond to him, so I only nod.

"No matter what happens...know that...know in your heart that you've been a good husband to Lucy." I know what he's not saying.

*If we don't find her. If she's...if.*

I only nod again. He gets up and quietly heads into the guest room.

I let out a long sigh though when I see Jake still standing on the terrace. It's just us now.

I walk out to the terrace quietly. Jake turns, but doesn't say anything. He's got the picture that I don't really want to talk to him.

But I know what else Dad was telling me; he won't let this go on much longer. I have to talk to Jake, get it over with.

**48** Her

I've been driving down the same road for a while. There are no lights, only a few houses. *I don't know where I am*. No streets, no signs look familiar. I've only sees fields of scrubby woods so far and patches of open fields. Is this Indiana? Michigan? I look for anything that I might recognize.

I see what looks like a semi-truck's lights on a road at a long distance to my left. *A main road? This one will have to intersect it eventually, right?*

I panic, taking gulps of air to calm. I lower the window, letting cold wind get the stench of Ben out of my nose again.

*Focus.*

*I only know a few things for sure.*

*I don't have clothes or money.*

*I have a nearly full tank of gas. Thank God. And I'm not stopping until it's out or I'm home.*

This gives me a thought.

*Ben said he'd been stalking me.* Going to my home and waiting outside my building for me for months. I look around and could almost slap my head if it wasn't still spinning. GPS. On the passenger side floor.

I pull over. I'm afraid of being spotted. Stopped. *But I have to know where I am, how to get the hell out of here!*

I plug the small box in. I could scream waiting for the stupid screen to light up and go through its happy dancing logo before getting to a menu.

I look in the mirror again. I'm unrecognizable even to myself. My eyes are crazy. A small part of my brain says that I must be in shock, hysterical, looney, la la…

*Finally! There it is.* My address. Already typed in. *Thanks, fucker!*

*Michiana. I'm close.*

I breathe a little slower, look around. No one is in sight. I don't know what time it is. His clock is broken. I think it must be after midnight. *Good. No one else on the road to see the crazy beaten up chick driving like a maniac.*

I don't know who Ben was or what he did. I do know small towns. *I want out of here.* I won't be stopped by some friend of his. He said he had lots of friends. I shake remembering how he said he would introduce me to them, as if we were a couple, like I'd never be anything but his. He laughed, saying he wasn't like Max. He liked to share his toys.

*Well, screw you, Ben! I'll run over any friend of yours I meet too. I won't be stopped.*

I put the car in drive and take off, fast. No stopping at lights or stop signs, only slowing down. The wheels are a hum that fills my brain, makes the numbness a song. *A crazy ass song*.

**49 Him**

I keep my distance. I can hardly look at Jake. I can feel my blood boiling at just the thought of him being here, with her. *Alone. Behind my back.* I need to take a moment to get over these thoughts. I need to see past this, somehow. "Jake." I don't know where to begin.

He does. "I'm sorry, Max. I messed up. I'm sorry for hurting you. I'm sorry for keeping anything from you. I…I only wanted to help." He's obviously been waiting to say all this, waiting to be alone with me. It's an avalanche of apologies.

I know he's sorry. I know he only thought he was helping. I've had enough time to think about this. But I still clench my fists and jaw at the reminder of Lucy keeping a secret from me. I let another deep sigh out.

"I know you did." His look of relief is almost comical, but I'm not letting him off the hook. "But you interfered in my marriage, Jake. I can't let that stand. I can't…" I swallow. Anger peaks. Pain plummets into my stomach. "I know you were trying to help Lucy. But you only confused her more. You added your own confusion over how we were raised…that wouldn't have helped her to come to terms with me, with us."

"I know…I know that now."

"You may not *like* it, brother. But Lucy *is* mine. And I won't allow you to interfere again." I feel better talking about a time when Lucy is with me once more. I can almost pretend that she's in our bedroom, crying after a good beating for her secrets. This is one of the thoughts I've been able to hold onto the longest, a fantasy that I can imagine even with a room full of people.

Jake's eyes spark at this, but his voice remains apologetic, "I won't try again. I…" He shrugs. "I get it…I guess…I talked to Dad." I nod. "But I already knew what he'd say. The same thing he's always said…that it was all for our own good. He talked about loving Mom, us. About how I didn't remember how…how bad she was to us, to herself before him. The same shit you've always said." He shrugs again and takes a seat. I stay standing, putting my hands in my pockets, fists still. "But then I talked to Mom."

I'm surprised. He's always acted so protective of her. We both have, not wanting to confront her about the past. I never thought he'd talk to her about his feelings over how Dad was with us, with her.

"She said all the same things. She cried." He runs his hands through his waves, just like mine, "She said she knew that I struggled more than you with how Dad was. But she hoped that I'd figure it out for myself. That tough love is still love. That's how she put it. The man would slap her right in front of us, and she loved him. He'd treat her like a child, sending her to their room...everything he did." He looks accusingly at me. "But she loved him. She said she's grateful that he came along. That she never knew what love and security was before him."

I want to hit him for making Mom cry, for making her explain this to him, for questioning everything, me, Dad, himself. But I'm fascinated too. I've never had the courage to talk to her about it, about her abuse or why she stayed with Dad. I know they love each other. *But there were times when I wondered...*

"She admitted to all the abuse you told me about. I even remembered a little hearing her talk..." His voice cracks at this admission. He's never really wanted to remember anything. "She apologized to me. Said that without Dad she doesn't know what she would've done...to us, to herself. That she was suicidal back then. Depressed. On and off using drugs and men to forget about the two boys she had at home who needed her." He looks at me with watery eyes. I didn't know this. I vaguely remember a lot of "uncles" and "special friends," but nothing specific.

"That's how she put it. She didn't hold anything back...maybe she's too raw over all this to hold anything back." He takes a deep breath. "But she told me that I need to stop blaming Dad. That she chose to stay. She chose to live by his rules, his discipline. That she's never regretted the life she has with him. And he's never really hurt her...not really. Just like he never really hurt us." He stands up to be inches from me. "And I know this much is true...I'm a stronger person because of Dad. Because of the love I had from Mom. And I know you protected me when I was a kid, Max. I'll do the same for you. Anything I can do to help, I will."

He waits for me to respond, but I only look at him. I can't bring myself to forgive him. Not yet.

"I'm sorry, Max. I won't interfere again. It's your business. I know you wouldn't ever really hurt Lucy. You love her. And she loves you."

I have to swallow to stop the tears I feel burning behind my lids. I can't say anything. I don't want to lose it, one way or another. I don't trust that I'll be able to stop myself from either beating the shit out of him or breaking down into a blubbering idiot. I can't do either right now. *I have to keep my shit together. For Lucy.*

Jake finally gets that I won't respond to him. He takes a step towards the door, only adding, "Lucy never would've left you. I know that now." I nod.

I finally sit when he walks down the hall to the front door.

I can't focus my thoughts for a moment. I have too many conflicting emotions. Anger being top on the list. I imagine beating the crap out of Jake. My rage over his betrayal almost suffocates me. I can't breathe for a moment. I have to stand, to pace.

I take my time fantasizing about having Lucy here now. What I would do to her for her betrayals. I smile at the image of her on her knees, begging me with tears. The beating I gave her once would be nothing in comparison to this amount of rage. It wouldn't just be once. I'd have her black and blue for weeks for what she's done.

I stop pacing though. *It's no use to imagine. She's not here. God help me, she may never be here again.*

This thought is more than I can take. With one small shudder, every tear I've held back is shaken loose. I stand in the cold with my hands at my sides, open, my head back, the tears not stopping. I can't control the emptiness I feel.

*I'd give anything to be able to hold onto the rage. To not feel this helplessness. But it's all I have. I'm lost without her.*

**50** Her

Even driving like a madwoman, it's taken a long time to get back. My limbs are stiff and heavy. My lids are hard to keep up. But there's my home. My city. My skyline.

The drive has given me time to think. Sort of. My mind keeps fragmenting.

Pictures pop of Max. Me. Us. But I can't put them in order. Today, tomorrow, yesterday, last week?

The fragment that won't stop flying across the windshield, my wicked witch on a broomstick…I'll get you and your snarling dog too…

Max's look of anger. That night. His angriest face. *The night I always go back to.*

It's filled my nightmares, my dreams, my days.

All because a man I barely knew touched my hand. That was enough to spark Max's rage. A rule broken. And I had to pay the price for that.

Even in a cage, I woke with that night in my head. Even with Ben's fists on me, I pictured that face.

I haven't admitted this to myself. Until I was free, there was no point in thinking about...

Max. My beautiful angry husband.

*How can I face you now?*

I *didn't let this happen...not like that night...I could've done something to stop Rich that night...should've done something...*

*But this...this is so much more, so much worse...Ben beat me, fucked me. Max will know this.* I laugh. *Everyone will know this. Just look at me...but Max won't be able to deal with this...he won't be able to control his anger...he won't be able to look at me the same way.*

Max is a man who has to be in control. I've known this almost since the beginning. *I've given him everything. But now? Now.*

I have to stop thinking for a minute, concentrate on the sound of the road, the lights and signs passing me. I have to blink away tears and swallow more air.

*Now. I'll never be the same again. Not to Max. Not to myself.*

*And…the part I've only let myself whisper, trapped in bed next to a monster…*

*I blame him. I blame Max.*

*I blame myself.*

*I blame Ben of course…but I ran* him *over.* I feel a strange smile on my lips at this thought. I touch my lips and it goes away.

I'm free. And trapped in a nightmare still.

I blink through the tears, not stopping them, *just need to see, dammit.*

A homeless man crosses out of nowhere in front of me. I have to slam on the brakes to avoid him. My forearms hit against the steering wheel. I don't feel the pain shooting up my arms. He curses at me, but keeps shuffling across the headlights with his cart of belongings.

I laugh. It's an awful sound. Harsh. High. Ugly. It's glass breaking in my throat laugh. I don't move. I just lower my head onto the steering wheel. And I cry. I'm almost home and I cry, finally.

I shake, cry, and sob. *God…another song of misery of crazy fucked up crazy ass shit goddamn and fuck!* More laughter trickles out of me.

But that helped. I look around again. Not a good place to stop, Lakeshore Drive. I can see a cop moving in my direction already. Even this late at night, it's still the tourist area.

I drive slowly away, not stopping when he waves me down. I have to get home. *My husband is waiting for me. God, help me…*

**51** Him

"Max!" Dad is yelling from the guest room. "Max! Get in here!" I've only just thrown my running shoes into the closet.

Since the crowd of reporters has been staying longer again, I've been running in the middle of the night. There's only a small group now that waits for me to return before giving up for good for the night. But avoiding the vultures isn't the real reason. I can't sleep and it's an excuse to work out my anger. I felt empty after crying, but it wasn't enough to exhaust me. Wasn't enough to stop my thoughts.

I throw my shirt into the closet too and start to walk out of my room. But the phone is ringing. *Shit*. I stop and grab the bedside phone. It's the lobby. "Mr. Traeger? I…I think…you should come down here, Sir. It's your wife…"

Dad is in my doorway. "The news! …I think Lucy's downstairs!"

My mind blanks for a second, piecing together what he means, what the call meant.

I don't bother with a shirt or shoes. I run out of the apartment. Dad's right behind me in his pajamas.

The elevator takes too long. We stare with open mouths at each other, both breathing hard, not speaking, frowning.

In the stark lobby, I take everything in in one blink. There's a small crowd of lights and cameras, and in the middle is my Lucy. Or what looks like my Lucy. She's trying to move through them towards the elevator, but I can see they're blocking the way. They keep asking their questions, pushing their mikes and lenses at her. Her hands are up and she looks frightened.

All my anger, fear, and pain tears out of me. I shove two cameras out of the way and punch another guy too close to her. She falls into my arms. Her lips barely breathe my name.

*My Lucy.*

## 52 Her

I don't need to open my eyes to know that I'm in a hospital room. The smell. The sounds. Beeps, hisses, muffled voices and footsteps, metal on metal clangs in a distance.

*Or am I back in the cage?*

I want to drift back to sleep. I don't want to open my eyes. I don't want to see his face. *Max. Ben.*

A single tear escapes my left eye, but I don't feel it until it drops onto my shoulder.

I drift. Thankfully, I drift.

**53** Him

"Lucy has a cracked rib, sprained wrist, fractured cheek, ruptured ear drum and a lot of cuts and bruises. She still has a low temp from an infection probably from the dog bites on her arm. She was severely dehydrated and in shock when I brought her in last night." It's barely 9:00 a.m., but time has slowed down, to the pace of doctors and nurses, coming and going, to police coming and going.

And this is about the fifth time I've had to say all this, to spell out the injuries my wife has. From another man.

Laura has her hand to her mouth, tears are in her eyes. She saw the early morning news. She's been calling me ever since. The reporters have swarmed the hospital, but we're able to keep Lucy's room private for now. I told Laura how to get up here without anyone noticing.

Dad, Mom, Liz, Paul, Jake, PJ…all are waiting in the family waiting room down the hall. So far, Lucy's been sleeping. She has tubes and monitors all over her. *My Lucy.*

"Can I see her?"

"Sure. But she hasn't been awake yet…"

"Of course." I push the door open to the room and let Laura go in alone. I can see Lucy's still body under the covers, propped up on the pillows. Her face is pale; the bruises are vivid.

I walk away before the door closes.

In the waiting room, all eyes turn to me. I only shake my head.

No one's talked to her. She passed out in my arms in the lobby and didn't regain consciousness even when the ambulance came. The doctors said she was in shock.

*So was I.*

She was a mess, bruised, bleeding, swollen. Naked. *Fucking naked under that dirty sweatshirt. With a fucking dog collar on.* Cuts up and down her legs, stomach, tits. *Blood between her legs. My Lucy.*

I didn't have to tell Dad what I wanted. He was on the phone arranging everything before I even had her on the bed. While I stayed with her, he took care of getting the rushed ambulance, private room for exam and care, and security against reporters and…whatever.

Now all I can do is wait. Wait for her to open her eyes again.

*My Lucy.*

*And for the police to tell me who did this to her...so I can kill them.*

## 54 Her

I feel a prick on my arm and moan. "I'm sorry, honey. You're still so dehydrated, your veins are hard to find."

A nurse is smiling at me. That's the first thing I see. Her hand presses on the inside of my left elbow. My left arm is white with bandages. Tubes come out of my left hand. I follow them up to a bag of clear liquid, back down. My right wrist is wrapped too. I swallow several times and she brings me a cup with a straw. Cool water hits my throat and I don't think I've loved the feel of anything more in my life.

I cough a little and she plumps up pillows behind me.

"Your family is going to be very happy to see your baby blues open, honey." She walks towards the door. "I'll get the doctor too." I want to tell her to stop. *Wait. Don't tell anyone that I'm awake...not yet. Please!*

But she's gone.

I close my eyes, but the solace of sleep is lost to me. I hold my breath waiting. I keep my eyes closed.

I can hear the door open. It's quiet but the sound from the hall gets louder for a moment.

"It's good to see you awake. How are you feeling?"

It's a stranger, a doctor. I open my eyes. He's youngish, smiling, looking at a chart. He's nice, clean cut. I vomit on him.

He steps back quickly and goes into the hall, "Nurse!"

But he returns to my side and pulls the sheets to cover the small amount of vomit on the side of the bed. He wipes my face and the front of my gown. I'm too weak to turn away from him. Too numb. He removes his jacket, leaving it on the floor without a care.

A nurse quickly comes in and he directs him to get a maintenance person in here right away, and to take my temperature. I watch all this silently.

Then he smiles at me again. *Nice.* I want to cry and apologize, but I stay silent. The movie goes on around me, but I'm not really in it. "Feel a little better?"

I only nod, but frown at the pain this causes. "Do you know where you are?" He puts a light on my eyes and directs me to follow it.

"In the hospital?" My voice cracks.

He picks up the cup and straw, and holds it for me. "Take small sips." I do, keeping my eyes on him.

"Yes. You were brought in early this morning. Do you know your name?"

"Lucy Traeger."

"Good. How about what day it is?"

I only shake my head, more frowning with pain. Time is fuzzy.

"You don't have a concussion, Lucy. You are still dehydrated though. And you have a small infection from the bite marks on your left arm. You've been running a temperature from it, but we're keeping this down."

Behind him the door opens again; this time it stays open longer. I stop drinking. I freeze.

*Max. Oh, God. Everybody*. I don't look at anyone. I look at the bed, with my wrapped up arms on the cover.

Max is by my side. His hand on the bed, where the vomit is hidden under the sheets. I start to retch again; my throat uncontrollably moves in long motions against my attempts to breathe. The doctor pushes Max aside and puts a dish under me just in time.

The doctor again wipes my face for me. I avoid looking at Max, but there's no missing his look. His angry look. I lean my head back and close my eyes again.

"I think we should let Lucy rest while we get her bed and gown cleaned up." The doctor directs everyone to leave.

"I'm not leaving." Max's voice, it's his strong, in control, edged voice. The doctor doesn't argue. *No one would argue with that voice.*

But Max stays against the wall. I only open my eyes enough to see him staring at me, but I pretend to have my eyes closed.

Two women come in and make quick work of moving me around the bed and getting it remade with fresh sheets and me in a fresh gown. I'm a ragdoll again, weak and powerless. I start to cry when they walk away.

Max is quick to be my side again, but I turn away from him before he can touch me. I roll over onto my right side ignoring the pain this causes. I turn into a ball and cover my face with the new sheet. I make no noise as I cry. I know he doesn't leave, but he doesn't touch me either. He stops at the end of the bed.

I finally stop crying, but I don't move the sheet away.

I can hear the door open again.

And I feel a hand on my shoulder. "Lucy? Sweetie?" *Mom.* I start to shake and cry again. I don't want to see her either. I don't want anyone to see me.

"Lucy, it's okay, sweetie." Mom's hand is soft, brushing my shoulder, "You're safe now. It's okay."

Her touch is gentle, but it feels like a live wire on me. I don't want to be touched. I move my shoulder to get her hand off of me, "Stop! I just want to be left alone…" It's a whine, a plea, a yell.

"Lucy..." Max's warning voice. *So familiar.*

I respond as I always do. Tingle. Pulse. *I want him. I want him, but...*

I move the covers and only let my eyes poke out. "I want to be left alone." This time my voice is more even, a little stronger.

I don't quite meet Max's eyes. I look at his chin. But his look darkens, his jaw sets, brow frowns. He even takes one step towards me. Then, he stops.

Mom only pats my shoulder and says, "Okay, sweetie. We're all here...whenever you're ready." She leaves squeezing Max's arm. His face has returned to neutral, but his eyes are still narrowed.

I don't say anything, just roll back over and pull the sheet up again.

Max doesn't leave. He stands there watching over me. I can feel his eyes on me, but I don't move.

A nurse comes in with meds. I don't ask what they are. I just take them with my eyes averted.

I don't roll over again, my side and wrist hurt too much, but I push into the bed more and close my eyes. Blocking out the site of Max's eyes on me.

*I can't face what he'll say. I can't face what I think.*

*I admitted to myself that I blame him. But I can never say that to him.*

*I can never say how sorry I am either. It would be no use. Sorry will never change what's happened, what I've been through. It won't change what Ben did.*

## 55 Him

Lucy won't open her eyes again for me. I don't say anything, just watch her.

*She turned away from me?* When I tried to comfort her. Tried to touch her. She turned away.

I still feel as helpless as I did when she was missing. I want to scoop her up and hold her close, never let go. But she looks so fragile. So broken.

Her breathing evens out briefly. She sleeps a little. But her body twitches, her little moans escape.

And I'm hard.

*I'm fucking hard. I'm sick. Looking at her, here, like this. But her little moans…I want to make them mine again. Just like in my dreams…beaten and mine.*

Instead she's beaten beyond recognition by another man. I have to stop my hands from clenching. I have to remind myself to remain calm. That the worst is over. Lucy's home. *She's where she belongs.*

*But she turned away from me.*

I've known fear in my life.

Fear that my deadbeat dad would or wouldn't come home. Fear that Mom wouldn't be able to stop herself once she started hitting me. Fear that I wouldn't live up to Ron's expectations and demands.

That brief but hot fear that Lucy would leave me once she knew the truth about me.

But the fear of the past ten days. I've not known this. It's a complete helpless fear.

I've been what society would call a victim before, as a small kid. Even then, something in me knew that I stayed because I chose to. I had to protect my little brother. I was more afraid for Jake than for myself. I even stayed for my mom. I knew she needed protecting too. She needed to be loved no matter what.

And the arrogant, cocky bastard in me always knew that I would be a success. That I'd have whatever I wanted. That I would be exactly what Ron wanted and more.

I've never felt helpless before, powerless. I always had choices. And I know that it's choices that give a person control.

*That's why I don't give Lucy any.* I *am in control. Of her. Of me.*

But not these ten days. And not now. She's choosing to keep herself from me.

*And I want to hurt her. For the fear. For the anger in me. For my lack of control. I want to punish her. But seeing her broken like this…I know I can't. I know the fear and helplessness again.*

*Mostly…I just want to hold her. Protect her. Make her safe again. Make her mine again.*

*I am a monster. And I don't care. I know who I am. Who she is. And she doesn't have the right to hide herself from me. Not ever.*

Her eyes flutter again and her breathing catches. I know she's awake, just keeping her eyes closed.

"Lucy."

Her eyes instantly open. *Good girl.*

**56** Her

His voice. The strong, deep voice I love. I crave. I need.

My name on his lips. A curse. A song. A dream?

I open my eyes. And for an instant I don't know anything. Just Max. His body. His eyes. His look.

His anger. And I respond. I moan.

But this brings back everything. Pain, confusion, fear, my own anger. I turn my head away.

His fingers turn my chin to him, but I stop whatever he's going to say. "Can you get a nurse for me?"

I don't meet his eyes. But he nods once and walks away.

*I can't do this! I can't be here. With him!*

All my thoughts…*that I'll never be what he wants again…that I blame him…that I was raped…Oh God.*

I start to cry. I can't get my brain to stop circling. *To focus or clear or whatever the hell I need.* I'm a drain, everything just keeps running out of me and away. I want to get away.

I'm moving off the bed, trying to stand. Tubes pull and things beep.

A nurse and that doctor come in quickly, followed by Max, Mom and Dad.

The doctor helps me to stand. Gently. "Do you need the bathroom, Lucy?"

I nod. He helps me to walk over to the door to a small bathroom, bringing my IV bag with me. "We'd like to get a urine sample; is there a receptacle in the toilet already?" The nurse nods to this. *This is so humiliating. I still can't use the bathroom by myself.* I moan in frustration and pain.

I close the door as much as I can with the IV monitor in the way.

When I come out, the doctor is gone, replaced by a new face. A short red-faced man in a crinkled suit now occupies his place.

The nurse helps me back into bed. I can't believe how stiff and sore I am. The smallest motions are making me whimper and hiss. My side is on fire. I can see Mom's face wince and Max's face set with a deeper shade of anger.

"I'll check with the doctor if we can give you anything for the pain, honey…" The nurse leaves.

All eyes stare at me. Max, Mom, Dad, and this new guy. Max hasn't softened his look. His eyes pierce me. I'm glad others are here now. I want to be alone, but I'm glad not to be alone with him. I can't face what he'd say, what I'd say.

"Lucy, I'm Detective Killaney." The short man smiles and looks awkwardly at my bandaged hands and arms, putting the hand he was offering to me back down. "I need to get a statement, if you're up for it."

Max steps in, "She needs her rest now, Killaney."

"I…I can…" My voice is small. Everyone looks at me though. No one else notices how Max's expression changes. Dark to darkest. I shudder. *A cardinal rule broken, contradicting him.*

"Good. We'd like to get everything down while it's still fresh in your head…" Killaney pulls up a chair next to my bed, making everyone move out of his way.

"Can you…Can you tell me if Ben…?" I can't help but see Max almost shake with anger behind the detective.

"How bout you give me all the details you can remember first…"

"Okay." I look at my hands on the cover, "Can…can we talk in private?"

I don't look up, but Mom and Dad turn quickly to leave, kissing my head as they go. They don't want to hear the details. I glance at Max; he only squares his shoulders and puts his hands in his pockets. "I'm not leaving, Lucy."

"Please?" My eyes swim with tears, but I don't look up again as I plead.

"If you want to do this now. Fine. But I'm not leaving." *It's his 'that's final' tone.*

I don't say anything else and Killaney settles back into his chair. "Why don't you walk me through last Friday…?"

I take a deep breath. I swallow thinking about how long ago it was. It was only ten days, but it was another life. *Another me.* "I left the house just after 1:30. When I got out of the cab in front of my doctor's office, I heard a man call my name. I thought it might…that Max might've come for the appointment. I turned and don't remember much after that. A blurry memory of being put into a car and the door slamming. I woke up in the trunk of Ben's car just before we got to his place."

I avoid looking at anything but my hands. My fingers press, pull, play, trying to distract me. My face is hot, breathing is hard. But my voice is surprisingly calm, detached telling these details.

I describe the beginning. When I figured out who he was, where I knew him from. I tell him that Ben said he'd stalked me for weeks at a time, but was going to give up. His lucky day, he said. No, I don't remember seeing him before that Friday. Just that one time in Italy.

My voice catches answering the detective's questions about Italy. "He said he noticed how I was with my husband.

He said he wanted that for himself." I don't add that he said I was already well trained for his tastes.

I describe getting away. *My* lucky day. How Bitch was hurt when he pushed me off the bed onto her. How he was drunk every night, but especially last night. How I ran, how I hit the dog, how I ran. How I drove over him. How I got home is a daze, but I made it.

I don't describe what he did to me though. *I can't.*

Killaney wants to know. Needs to have everything out, to write everything down.

I finally take one more deep breath in. *If I say it fast, maybe I can get it all out...*

"Ben was hot or cold. One minute he'd be quiet and kinda nice. The next he'd hurt me. With his fists, boots, belts, rope, spatulas, newspapers, a small wooden figurine thing he had by the bed, whatever was within reach." I itemize this like a grocery list, trying to push away the memory of every item in his hands, on my body.

"He kept me in Bitch's cage when he left for work, and on a leash, with a small choke collar when he was home." I rub my hand over the small bandage on my throat. I don't know what happened to that. "The dog...kept me from getting loose. Those teeth." I shudder. But that unfamiliar smile takes over my lips again. I cover it with my hand. "She won't be using her snarling teeth again on me..."

Killaney shifts in his seat. I'm brought out of my strange memory of the impact of dog, skillet, and arm.

I continue in the same small, quiet, calm voice. Only by saying it fast can I get through this. I close my eyes. "Ben raped me. Several times each day. I lost track of how often. My mouth, my cunt, my ass…" *Ben's words.* I can hear his voice in my head, next to my ear. His ugly words, making me say them, making me beg with his words.

I hear Max's feet move closer to the bed, feel the bed shake. But I don't open my eyes. *I can't.*

## 57 Him

The words are embedded in my brain. Drugged. Trunk. Beaten. Caged.

*Hearing what he did. To my Lucy. Anger is too small. Rage is too weak. Insanity…that fits.*

I have to control my breathing, to keep my hands from shaking. I try to stay as calm as Lucy sounds, for her sake. But Killaney doesn't stop the details.

Her words again echo in my head. *Raped.* I didn't have to be told this. I saw her. I knew. *But hearing it…*

I wish I could take away all her pain, all her memories. I wish I could make it so she never has to say these words again, that she couldn't even remember them.

I'm almost numb with the fathom of hate and anger, with the uncontrollable need to kill.

And in my well of darkest red, she curses. I'm shocked out of my numbness. Hearing those words come out with her sweet voice. *Cunt. Ass. A rule she knows well.* But she sits there, speaking so calmly.

It was the first lesson I taught her. It was the start to our understanding, our way of being together. *And here, now, she calmly breaks my rule?!*

I don't think, I just move towards her. My hands are out of my pockets. It's not the cop sitting next to her though that stills me, stops me from punishing her.

It's her. Her face. Her arms. Her hands. She's broken, too like how she was in my dreams after I'd given in to my rage and beaten her.

And she's not here. She's not with me. She's hiding again…in her memory of what he did to her. *She's ruled by another. In her head, she's still his prisoner.*

I squeeze the end of the bed with my hands, shaking it in my anger. Killaney glances at me and I slowly pull my hands back.

Lucy finally opens her eyes and looks right at me this time. But she's hidden behind that mask, again; it's a calm, cold, dead mask. "That's everything, Detective. Everything I can think of right now…"

Killaney pats her bed, not touching her, but close. "You did just fine, Lucy. I'll let you get some rest now." He stands to walk out, but she stops him.

"What…what happened to Ben?"

He looks at me, then turns to her. "We were able to track his address down from the car registration and GPS. Local police found him just as you described, still on the driveway. He died while in surgery about two hours ago."

She smiles that same eerie smile, not one I've ever seen on her sweet face. *Not one I ever want to see again.* "And Bitch?"

"His dog. They haven't found her yet."

Lucy nods, still smiling. She finally closes her eyes again, but the smile stays.

I walk with Killaney out to the hall.

"Your wife was very brave." I only nod. "What she described…getting away like that…" He shakes his head. "I'll have to get a few more details later, but I think this will wrap up pretty quick. We have enough evidence between what we found in his car, the house, on Lucy." He pauses, looking apologetically at me. "And he's dead, so…" He shrugs and turns to walk away.

I don't go back into her room. I give her some time to sleep. *And I need some time to think.*

## 58 Her

"You get some sleep, sweetheart." Dad kisses my head. It hurts, but I manage not to wince. PJ and Cathy just left a few minutes ago.

Mom finally stopped crying. She even tried to make a few jokes and complain about the hotel room. She kisses my hand and promises to be back first thing in the morning, to call her cell if I need her at all during the night. I promise I will. I know I won't.

I almost roll my eyes when Alex and Ron walk in the barely closed door.

Ron sees my exasperation. His look is stern, but his voice is soft. "We're not staying, Lucy. Just want to say goodnight. You get your rest. We'll be back in the morning." I smile and say goodnight too. I try not to wince at their small touches and Alex's kiss.

I've had too many people all looking at me. Too many nurses and doctors poking at me. Not enough time to myself. To think.

Max has been in and out, but we haven't really spoken. He's been here every time the doctors check on me, every time someone comes in to talk to me.

Dad told me that Max has private security on the floor to keep anyone not on a list out of my room. The hospital doesn't like it, but they don't want the negative publicity of a victim being harassed in one of their rooms by the press or anyone.

*A victim. That's me. Kidnap victim. Rape victim. Assault victim….blah blah blah victim.*

*I'm also a murderer.* I smile again. *I like that word more.*

*Ben won't be bothering me again. Accept in my dreams…* So far he's been in a lot. *But maybe I'll just have to run him over again and again a few times before he goes away for good...*

Only a few minutes go by before a new vampire comes in for my bloodletting and turns the lights up. My fever has stayed down, but apparently they're still worried about the effects of dehydration. I still have an IV with saline and a cocktail of stuff.

When she leaves, I lower the lights myself and close my eyes. Maybe I can get to sleep before Max comes in again.

*Nope. No such luck.*

He moves quietly.

"I know you're not asleep, Lucy." I debate about ignoring this. But I know I can't.

I open my eyes and he touches the tips of my fingers. It's the one spot that doesn't seem to hurt. But it's an electric feeling. Our touch always is. I pull my fingers away.

"I know you've been through a lot, Lucy. So I'm going to give you some time…and some space. To heal." He keeps his fingers flat on the bed, but I can see that his other hand is a fist at his side. He's trying to keep his voice softer, but the low rumble of his rage is just below the surface. "But know this, little girl, that I'm not giving you this space to act however you'd like. I may not be able to punish you right now, but that doesn't mean I'll let you get away with anything either."

He doesn't wait for my response. He leans over and kisses just below my right eye, another spot that isn't throbbing with pain. And he leaves without another word.

I know he's not leaving the hospital. He'll be right down the hall and he'll be checking on me.

I start to cry again when the door closes.

My body is too fragile right now for my mixed up feelings. I sob once loudly, but I'm afraid of being heard. Afraid that someone will come in. I grab my pillow and shove my face in it.

I have the familiar response to his anger. His warnings. *I am his little girl. I want so much to be his good girl again.* I long for a time when Max could simply erase everything with his hand or belt. When he'd turn his disappoint in me into my pain and I'd earn his forgiveness and love.

It seemed so hard to make that choice once, to give myself to him completely, to allow him full control. I'd go back to those days...of only worrying about disappointing him if I was late or didn't finish a chore. I'd go back to the days of fearing that I couldn't meet his demands, that I couldn't take his anger, that I couldn't make him forgive me.

*I'd go back to being able to earn his forgiveness. Back to when he didn't need to earn mine.*

I'd go back to being naïve of real rage and evil.

*But now*? I shudder thinking about Ben. *I wear his marks on me now. Maybe always.* I have cuts and broken bones that will forever be marked by another man.

*I'll never be Max's good girl again. Ever.*

I sob louder. *I'm sorry, Max!*

## 59 Him

I open the door to the family waiting area. I feel like a caged animal in here, but it's the only place to go to be alone right now. I'm not leaving here without Lucy. I'm not going back to our apartment without her. I won't leave her alone here.

I know she's safe. I've made sure of that. I'll make sure of that for the rest of her life. She'll never be alone again, never be vulnerable again.

But I can't leave her here. She needs me even if she doesn't want to admit it, even if she's hiding behind her calm mask. *I know my little girl*. She's broken inside in more ways than one.

When Killaney said that bastard was dead...I still wanted to have his body. To beat the shit out of it. To rip it apart, limb by limb. To watch it burn into a million pieces of ash and then step through it. Piss on it. *Fuck*.

"FUCK!"

"Oh…hey…" I turn with fists raised. The blanket in the corner chair moves, revealing a guy.

I lower my fists, but keep them clenched. I didn't see him in here. He wasn't in here earlier today. He rubs his eyes, yawns, and says loudly, "Sorry about startling you. I thought I was the only one sleeping here tonight."

He puts his hand out, but I ignore this. I don't feel like being friendly. Too many people have already invaded my space and time with Lucy. I need to be alone and to think more. He only smiles and lowers his hand.

"I'm here for my wife. She was in an accident…"

*Good for you. Fuck off.* I don't say anything. "Doctors say she'll be fine, but they had to do surgery on her collar bone. She's been pretty out of it. How bout you?" He yawns and stretches. I only look at him. "Who are you here for?"

I move a little closer to him, not letting my fists go. "Sorry to hear about your wife. But I'm not here to make a new friend. If you don't mind. Fuck off."

He blinks at me several times. But he slowly gets up and leaves the room.

I sit, putting my head in my hands. *I gotta keep it together. I can't lose my temper here. Just a little longer.*

I need to think through what do with Lucy. How do I get her out of this strange state? She won't talk to me. She's avoided even looking at me.

*And go ahead...you can say it to yourself...she's not behaving. Not like she should. Not like she did.*

*She contradicted me, talked back, cursed...just short of argued with me this morning in front of that fucking doctor that keeps touching her.*

*How do I handle this? How do I give her what she needs while she's healing without losing my temper with her?* I've come so close to slapping her today...two, three times already. Only all the bandages and her swollen face have stopped me.

*I don't want to admit that...that I'm afraid.*

*What if. What if this mess has changed my Lucy? Can I change her back? Get her back?*

*Fuck!* I'm sick of feeling helpless, powerless.

*Tomorrow. I'll start tomorrow.* My instincts have always been right with her...*I just have to trust them now.*

*I'll get her back and never let her go again.*

## 60 Her

I moan when the light goes on. I only just started to fall back asleep after a nightmare. Ben was running Max over with me in the trunk. I tried to scream, to warn Max to get out of the way. When I was fully awake I could think how odd dreams are that even though I was stuck in the trunk, I had a perfect view of both Ben and Max.

I wait for the cold hand on my arm, the prick of the needle again. But it's the doctor from earlier. *The nice one.* I haven't seen him since this morning.

"Hi, Lucy. How are you feeling?"

"Fine. Thank you."

He smiles. He has a kind, nice smile. I want to tell him not to waste it on me. "Your heartrate was elevated. Are you getting any sleep?"

I only shrug.

"Hmm...You know we've been running a lot of tests on you since you've been here...?"

I lift my right arm showing the needle pricks and bruises on the inside. They're tiny in comparison to all my other marks. "Sorry about that..." I only shrug. "Your latest blood work is good. Your potassium is back up. We'll get this IV out of you soon." He smiles again, "I should be able to release you later this morning." I try to smile at this, but it's fake, forced.

"I...I know that you have a lot of support here...your family and friends, your husband...but when a person..." He swallows. This is obviously not his usual conversation with a patient. "You should consider talking with someone, getting some help with everything that's happened to you. I could recommend a few doctors if you'd like...?"

I smile. It's a small smile, but genuine one this time. His kindness and awkwardness make me want to cry for some reason, but I smile instead. "I'll think about it. Thanks."

"I'll have instructions for you to follow up with your doctors. And how to take care of your arm and wrist...and rib...well, everything I guess." He looks me up and down, with a concerned frown. I know I still look like crap. I'm a mummy of bandages and wrappings right now. I only say another small thanks. "Call the nurses' station if you need anything at all...or if your husband has any questions for me..."

I know Max has been questioning everything. The nurses have all told me how lucky I am to have such a devoted and caring husband.

The doctor walks away quietly. I know I won't be sleeping again anytime soon.

Thinking of going home…I don't know what I feel or think. I want to lie to myself, to say that everything will be fine. *Max will be the same. I'll be the same. Everything'll be the same.*

*But I'm not. It won't. He won't.*

*It was only ten days of my life.* I laugh thinking this. I try not to think about everything that happened. What Ben did to me.

But I keep startling myself with a quick image or memory. A doctor's shiny pen will remind me of Ben's shiny knife. The sound of a metal cart being pushed in the hall will remind me of the cage door clanging closed. Turning in my sleep, I'll feel my rib ache and remember why.

*And it's funny…I know myself too well to shrink from this truth…I know that as awful as it was…I'll get over it. The physical part anyway.*

*I was raped. And I can get over that. I don't know how. I just know it's true. Maybe killing the bastard that did this to me helps.* I can feel the same smile take over my face at this thought.

The nurses and doctors have all looked with such pity on me. I'm sure I'm the whispered story in the hallways. I haven't even dared to turn on the news. I'm the poor girl that was kidnapped and all sorts of evil done to…

But that's not what has me thinking, worrying.

*I'll get over the pain that Ben caused me. The parts of my body that he still controls now with his pain...they'll be mine again, hopefully...*

*What I can't get over is the thought that Ben came into my life for those ten days because of a stupid impulsive move on my part. To please Max. To show him just how willing I am to be what he wants.*

I watched a show once, a reality series, about a guy who would visit normal people and shake up their lives, giving them a wakeup call to make a change for the better. It was a crappy show. But I always felt sorry for the people, that they obviously needed to make a change, but they were too dumb to see it until some idiot came along to tell them.

*I killed Ben, the idiot that shook up my life.* I laugh. *What a non-melodramatic way to put it! Laugh or cry? Neither, please...*

I hold my breath until I can blink without tears. I breathe in and out a few more times, just concentrating on this.

*I killed Ben. I'm glad he's dead. He was a worthless piece of shit and he deserved to die. There. Done.*

*Hopefully done.* But I don't kid myself about this either. He'll be a frequent flyer in my dreams and thoughts for a long time coming. *But he's dead at least.*

I need to figure out what it is that I want. *This shaken up wakeup call change to my life...what is it?*

*Max.* He's filled my every thought practically since we met. I haven't questioned my love for him. How I respond to him. *That night he hurt me so badly...*

*Nothing like Ben.*

No, that's true...but he did hurt me. On purpose. In anger. Max loves me and he punishes me. I've accepted this. I'd given up even questioning it...except in secret with Jake.

I haven't seen Jake. Alex told me that he'll see me soon, but he didn't want to have a big crowd here. I don't know what to think of that. I've gotten pretty close to him the past few months. I heard his voice in my head in the cage too, telling me to have hope and faith in Max, that I'd be found.

I shake my head. I need to concentrate on Max...*what am I supposed to do? I wish he could tell me...*

*Can I go back to that? Can I go back to listening to his every word, his every rule? Can I be the girl who Ben met in Rome?*

*How do I forgive him?*

He's why I was there, why Ben noticed me in the first place. I've forgiven everything else that Max has done. *No. I've not even had to forgive...I've given him permission, given him myself.* He could do what he pleased and I would take it. Ever since that first time he slapped me...even before then when he started to take control...I've been his.

I feel the familiar pulse deep in my pussy. Just thinking about Max in this way, I feel a warmth.

*Am I sick?* Should *I get help?*

I should get some sleep, but I know damn well that isn't going to happen. My voice in my head is even different. I never cursed this much…*is this in rebellion against Max? Against his rules?*

My head spins with the ways only ten days has changed me, my life.

*What do you want, Lucy?* Pretend it's Jake asking…how would I answer?

*He would tell me to stop talking to myself like a crazy person.* I stick my tongue out in the darkness and smile. A small part of me is in here somewhere, right?

I take a deep breath.

*I* want Max. I can analyze this until I'm blue, but that is the truth. Fight it. Don't. In the end, I want Max. But I have no idea how to make that happen now.

Will he be able to forgive me? I will forever bear the marks of another man. I know this is important to him. He likes to see me with a bruise or welt after he's punished me, to remind me of his control, that I belong to him. Will he be able to still look at me the same now with Ben's marks on me? Feel the same? I had this thought when I was alone in Ben's car…driving crazy to get away, to get home.

In a bloody, beaten state I worried about how Max would feel when he saw me. *He'd know. Right away he'd know that…what Ben did.*

I can't think anymore. *I just want to stop thinking!* Isn't there a pill for this? I'll invent one…

*It's only been ten days. Nothing has to change. Everything can be fine…right? Right.*

I turn the TV on mute. No news. I don't see what's on through my tears, but I don't feel as alone with its light.

## 61 Him

"I wasn't sure what all to bring, so I grabbed a few things just in case." Mom hands me a small bag filled with Lucy's stuff. I'd asked her to pick up some clothes since the doctor said Lucy will be released this morning. I glance down and see sunglasses on top. *A good idea.*

I'm pretty sure our building is still a zoo of reporters. I've seen Eve and Killaney on the news giving reports. I've seen coverage of the house in Michigan. I've avoided seeing too much of that. I don't need details in my head to go along with the rage I still feel.

The reporters will go away soon, but they haven't been able to get near Lucy since she stumbled into the lobby. They want a statement, the details of her horror story. *Not gonna happen.*

Mom follows me back into Lucy's room. Liz sits on the bed and nods towards the bathroom. "She's changing." I raise an eyebrow to this. Lucy didn't have anything but that sweatshirt and the police took that as evidence. "I got her something to wear from the gift shop downstairs…"

I only nod. *She should've asked me.* Lucy opens the door and I frown. She's wearing an oversized hoody and sweatpants with flip flops. I let it go for now though. She tries to smile at all of us.

"I was finally able to brush my teeth." Liz and Mom give a small laugh to this, but I can see the pain on Lucy's face.

"You sure you don't want a wheelchair for getting out of here, baby?"

"I'm sure. Thanks." She looks at the bag I'm holding. I pull out the sunglasses and she smiles, and says again in her small voice, "Thanks."

She moves slowly with the rest of us walking near. The two security guards meet us at the elevator. Lucy only frowns at them, but doesn't say anything.

The mob around the building is as bad as I thought it would be. The two guards come in handy, clearing a path for Lucy, getting her safely into the elevator without contact from anyone. Jeff helps too. The guards stay outside our door, but he follows us in.

Killaney already told me that the sad truth about stories like ours is the repeat attacks or attempts. That some freak out there gets it in their head that they know Lucy from the news and would want to get close to her. *Not gonna happen.*

Lucy won't be without security ever again. I arranged with Jeff to hire a group of his ex-cop friends, as security and additional drivers. *No one's going to get close to my Lucy unless I say they can.*

She stands around the living room, just taking everything in. Mom has the place clean and put together. I try to see what Lucy's seeing. Her eyes are filled with tears, but she doesn't move.

"Why don't you lie down, baby?"

"No. I'm going to take a shower…" She moves quietly towards the bedroom and shuts the door.

"How bout I make us all something to eat for lunch?" Mom is already heading to the kitchen.

But Paul stops her, "Why don't we four go out and bring something back for the kids?" He smiles sadly at me. I nod.

Dad nods and Mom just quietly grabs her purse. Liz is upset though, "I think we should all be here…just in case."

She hasn't spoken to me about her accusations. We haven't talked about my spanking Lucy or telling her to mind her own business. I know she's still upset. I don't say anything. *She's Paul's wife. Let him handle her.* I nod to Jeff and he heads out the door.

Then I turn to follow Lucy into the bedroom. I hear everybody else walk down the hall and close the door. *Good.*

I didn't want to be rude, but I've had enough of people around. I'm sure Lucy has too. *I need some time with my wife. Alone. To straighten her out.*

The bathroom door is closed. *She knows better. Maybe she closed it because our parents are here?* But in the back of my mind...*she's been pushing me. Pushing her limits. Why? On purpose or because she's in this strange shocked-state still?*

*If it's on purpose, is it because she can get away with it? Or* thinks *she can anyway? She thinks I won't do something because her parents are here or because she's hurt? Because she wants to see how much I'll let her get away with now? Because she* wants *me to be angry with her? Because* she's *angry and acting out?*

I clench my fists tighter.

*If it's this shocked blank state of mind, how do I get her out of it? Will she come out of it on her own, with time and patience?*

*Fuck.* I don't know what's going on in her head. I've always been able to tell exactly what Lucy's thinking. She's always been so expressive and open to me.

I turn the knob and it's locked. I can hear the shower running. I don't pause. I've been too on edge, restraining myself for too long. I bust the door open in one strong punch with my shoulder.

Lucy screams and stands. She wasn't in the shower yet; she was just sitting next to the tub. And she was crying.

"You know better than to lock this door, little girl."

She doesn't move or speak. Her face moves quickly from fear and guilt to freeze into that same blank look she's been wearing. Her eyes are still red from crying, but no tears now.

"Answer me, Lucy."

Her breathing labors, her whole body shakes with the effort to breathe and swallow. When she finally speaks, it's a tiny sound, but it echoes in my head, "Please…get out."

It takes me a second to realize what she said. It halts me for a moment, staring at her. I take in her blank look, her hard breathing, her shaking body. *Her broken body and face.*

*Fuck. I can't. I can't do this. Not now.*

But I take a step towards her anyway. I'm running on emotions and instinct. My brain is telling me to turn away and give her space, but my heart won't listen. My body won't listen.

She takes a step back and stops at the tub's edge, but she meets my eyes. She crosses her arms and tries to look strong. But she's still blank. Her eyes are blank.

"What did you say to me?" I put everything into this simple question. All my anger, my fear, my pain, I tremble with each word. My voice bounces off the marble, hurting my own ears. I didn't yell, but it fills the room.

And something flashes in her eyes. Something like my Lucy. A hint that she's still in there somewhere. She lowers her eyes, but keeps her arms crossed.

"I'm sorry…can I have some privacy? I don't want you to see me…" She has a blank tone to match her blank eyes, turned back up to meet mine again.

"Keep the door open." I turn and leave. I sit on the bed, rubbing my hands through my hair.

*Fuck*!

## 62 Her

*I have an entourage.* That's what it feels like. A full brigade of people. Mom, Dad, Ron, Alex. Max. And his henchmen. I didn't expect to see bodyguards. Or Jeff.

I listen to the sounds around me. Mom keeps trying to get me to talk, but I can't. I'm numb. I only smile slightly at her. *Please, shut up, Mom.* When we get to our building, I'm grateful for the bodyguards. They keep the reporters and cameras out of my way.

*Thank God. I didn't even think about them being here.*

When I got here in the middle of the night...it seems a dream, a nightmare...I hardly remember anything. The lights, the questions, the people pushing and pulling. And then Max. His strong arms, his shocked face.

Today, the people are kept back. I can breathe. No one can swarm.

And I'm almost happy. Numb and relieved.

Until we get inside. The two bodyguards stay outside the door. *Are you kidding me...are they here to keep me in?! What do they need to keep out? I killed Ben.*

I shudder thinking of this. Mom is oblivious. She's trying to touch me and I keep moving away, further into the apartment.

But I can't help thinking...*nothing's changed, but everything's changed!*

I look around and I can tell that it's been cleaned and straightened. Probably Alex. But it no longer feels safe. No longer feels like home.

I head into the bedroom, closing the door against all the people. My family, my husband...I don't want to be near any of them right now.

I want to break down. I want to have a breakdown, quietly, by myself.

I close the bathroom door and without thinking, lock it. I keep my hand on the door. *Max won't like this if he finds out.* I hesitate, *should I unlock it?*

*No. I need to be alone. He can wait to say whatever he wants to say to me.* He's been trying to be alone with me, to talk to me. I don't know what I should say, what I want to say. I'm too tired to form anything coherent right now.

I turn on the shower. I really need one. I start to take off the bandages and wraps. I stop when I take off the first bandage on my left arm. Bitch's teeth marks are inflamed, white and red, puffy and sore.

I have to sit down. No tears fall, but I just stare at my arm through a watery film. *I'll always remember this. I'll never be able to put it completely behind me, because I'll always see these scars and I'll always remember the feeling of her mouth cracking on the skillet. The feel of Ben on me...I may someday get over it, but I'll never completely forget.*

I hear the doorknob turn and wait for Max to demand that I open the door. I jump up and scream when he bangs in instead. He's furious, but he stops. He just looks at me. *I know what he sees. I'm broken, not his wife. Not his.*

I almost respond automatically to his angry voice, but my brain and heart are at war. Brain wins; I ask him to leave. I know I'm in trouble, but I can't stop my brain train on its tracks to self-destruction now. And amazingly, Max leaves.

I start to shake and cry. *I almost wanted him to hit* me. I'm not sure I could hurt any more than I do right now. But he only walked away... *I was right. He doesn't feel the same about me. He only sees a broken girl. He knows I'm not his anymore...that I can't be.*

I said I didn't want him to see me and that's true. *I don't think I can stand naked in front of him, not with all this.* I look at my arm again and rip off the rest of the bandages. Up and down my arm are the same red angry teeth scratches and tears. My right wrist is looking less swollen, but it's almost black with bruises. I yank off the hoodie and sweatpants. I tear off the wrap around my ribs. *I'm black and blue all over.*

I stare at myself in the mirror. *I don't know this girl. She's not me. I belong to Max. She doesn't.*

It takes me a long time to pull my eyes away and step into the shower. I don't move under the water. Just let it run its course over me. When it starts to cool down, I finally wash myself. This doesn't give me any relief, but I do feel better. Washing away the final remnants of Ben and Bitch, I do feel better.

I take my time drying off. I have to be gentle. I put the wrap around my ribs and wrist back on. My robe isn't in here. So I put the hoodie and sweatpants back on too.

I stop though, seeing the candle on a side table. The same candle I stared at for ten days. I watch my hands pick it up and throw it into the trash. I don't shed a tear, but I can feel my heart tearing.

Max looks up when I walk quietly out of the bathroom. He looks like he's been crying. I want to put my arms around him, tell him it'll be okay. I want his arms around me, telling me the same.

But we only stare at each other. Finally, his eyes narrow, "You're not wearing that."

I look down at myself. The clothes hang on me and the sweatshirt rubs my arm. I don't say anything, just walk over to the closet and open the door to see what I can put on. I pull a long skirt and long sleeve t-shirt and walk back to the bathroom to change. I leave the door open though.

When I come back out, Max isn't sitting on the bed anymore. He returns quickly though with the bag from the hospital. He pulls out gauze and bandages. "I'll help you put these on."

I only take them quietly, "No…I can do it...thank you." *He can't see me.* I quickly go back into the bathroom and cover my left arm with multiple strips of bandages. I'm the mummy again. The rest of the cuts I think are okay to leave alone. The doctor only gave me instructions for caring for the bite marks and cracked bones.

I avoid looking into my eyes. I know my face is a mess. My left eye feels like it's swimming and my right ear feels like it's filled with cotton. I don't need to see myself anymore.

Max hasn't left the bedroom. *I guess he's ready to talk.* I just wait.

"Come here." Max has his stern look, the warning look. His voice is the beautiful rich deep one I love. I respond without thinking about it. I stand in front of him, my head down, wet hair cooling my face, but my eyes are on his. "We need to talk." I nod slightly. "*I* need to talk and *you* need to listen."

He hasn't touched me. *I haven't had a physical connection with him in how long? Too long...* But I don't reach for him. I can't. I couldn't take his rejection.

"You're pushing my limits, Lucy." His voice takes on the edgier, angrier tone. "Why?"

I open my mouth, but I can't think of what to say to him. How to explain everything in my head. *I'm too afraid that he'll say out loud that he can't love me the same.* I only close my mouth and shake my head.

"Answer me, little girl."

I still only shake my head. Two trains on a headlong collision course…*touch me, hit me…stop, leave me alone.* He doesn't do anything.

He sighs and puts his hands on his knees. "While you're healing, I won't punish you." *I knew he didn't see me the same.* "But that doesn't mean that I'm not keeping an eye on you. You'll get the rest you need. But you'll keep track of the rules you've broken." His look darkens even more, so familiar that I want to cry and beg him to make me his again. "What rules did you break already today, little girl?"

I shake my head, but my voice is automatic. *The well-trained puppy in me, I guess.* "I didn't dress like you like. And I locked the door."

"Good. Get your journal and write those down." I don't move. I wait for him to get up, but he doesn't move either. "Now!" I jump at the roar and move towards my nightstand. I keep my running log in the drawer.

Opening the journal, I look at my handwriting, the numbers, and my eyes blur. "I ran."

Behind me, his voice sounds startled, "What?"

"I ran….I ran fast…because you made me run…all these hours…" I hadn't thought of this before. I heard his voice in my head telling me to run. I heard his voice in the woods. I heard his voice above the sound of Bitch behind me.

But seeing the times and distances I recorded for him, I know that I wouldn't have been able to run that fast, I wouldn't have gotten away if it weren't for training to run with Max. If he hadn't ordered me to start training all those months ago.... "I got away from Ben and Bitch…"

"Don't say those names again, Lucy." And he gets up and walks out.

I'm left alone, with only my tears and thoughts to keep me company finally.

*I got away because of you, Max. You stayed in my head. Your voice told me what do, how to survive, how to get home to you. I ran because I could, because of you. And now I've lost you anyway.*

But I don't say any of this. I don't follow him. I only sit down and right the rules on a clean sheet of paper. I ignore the pain in my wrist.

Somewhere…deep…I'm starting to feel something again though.

*I blame Max, myself. But without him…I wouldn't have survived…wouldn't have escaped. I wouldn't be able to sit here calmly writing after everything that happened.*

*Max is my stability. My life. I long for his touch…I don't care if it's rough or tender…I am his.*

*But I know that he doesn't feel the same…he probably never will.*

One tear plops on the page and bleeds the ink. *Will he ever see me the same way again?*

## 63 Him

It's late. I'd sent Lucy to bed hours ago. She didn't argue at least. I take another sip of scotch. I need to try to get some sleep, but I know it's no use. I don't want to wake her, so I'll probably sleep in the guest room tonight if I sleep at all.

*Today was rough. For everyone.*

Liz kept trying to smother Lucy. Paul kept trying to get her to back off. Mom and Dad tried to stay out of the way. Jake thankfully didn't come around at least. I don't think I could take seeing them together right now.

*Lucy…she walked around like a zombie. She wrote in her journal. I got her to do that much. It's a start.*

I'd decided to go back to basics with her. To start over, like when we first met. Reciting my rules, fearing my anger…*it's a start.*

I don't know if this'll work, but I can't just do nothing. I can't let that fucking monster destroy us. She looks so fragile now. Like she'll snap any second and not ever be the same.

Dad's right. I need to give her space. It's not what I want to do. I want to go in there right now and take her. Show her that she still belongs to me and make her stop thinking about anyone or anything else.

*Hearing her talk about him and his fucking dog. The details of everything. Fuck.* I look at my empty glass. *Not going to help.* I put it on the glass table and walk closer to the edge of the terrace. The night air is still cold, but it feels good.

It was cold that night Lucy escaped. She was freezing in my arms, her hands and legs like ice, blue from cold and bruises. I want her to know that she'll always be safe, that I'll never let anything happen to her ever again.

· I should've kept her safer. I want to tell her that she'll never leave my side again, that she'll stay locked in here, my private possession. I'm tempted to make this her tower. I even told Dad this. He laughed and said he knows how I feel, but that it would only harm her in the end.

I asked him if there was ever a time when Mom was unsure of herself and him, when she wasn't behaving. He laughed at this too. Said there were plenty of times, especially in the beginning. He told me that it was when he needed to be his most strict and demanding with her.

But he reminded me again that he doesn't think that's what Lucy needs right now. He and Mom never had to go through something like this. He was uncertain of what I *should* be doing, but made me promise to give Lucy time.

I just wish I knew what Lucy was thinking. She won't let me in.

Maybe she does need to talk to someone.

If she won't talk to me, maybe I can get her to talk to someone else, to open up about what she's thinking. How she's feeling.

Maybe I can get her to admit why she's pushing me away. Maybe I can get her to give me some insight into how I can pull her back.

*Fuck! I'll do anything for her. But this is hard to swallow…having to ask for help with her.*

## 64 Her

"Hey! You're downstairs?" I buzz Laura into the building and open up my front door. The two towering men turn to look at me.

"Ma'am?" The shorter one always speaks first.

"My friend is coming up here." I feel oddly defensive. I'm not sure if he'll argue with me, on some orders from Max or something. He only nods and turns again to face the hallway.

Max finally went into the office today. It's Friday. He has his staff meeting. PJ took Mom and Dad to the airport early this morning. *I guess life is supposed to go back to normal now.* Only two weeks ago I was a kidnapped victim. Today, I'm grounded. More or less.

Max didn't tell me I'm being punished, he just stationed two bodyguards outside our door. And Max won't let me leave

the building. He said this in front of them before he left this
morning. "My wife isn't to leave the apartment today." I
expected them to click their heels and raise their arms in
salute.

I laughed at first, picturing what these two would do to
keep me in here. But the truth is, I don't want to leave. I don't
want to face the world just yet. I still look like crap.

Waiting for Laura, I look in the mirror and push my hair
a little more forward on the left. Blood vessels are still shot,
but the skin has faded a little. A few of the scabs on my neck
are gone, just bright red scars now. I have bright red scars
everywhere, except my arm. The deeper gashes are still open
with bandages to cover them.

Laura pushes the door open and comes in, giving me a
big hug, but stops when I wince from my rib. She ignores this
though. I already told her on the phone yesterday that I'm tired
of how much my mom babied me while she was here. "Who
are the hotties outside?"

"My watchdogs." I had started to laugh, but calling them
this…*too close to what Bitch actually was*…I stop and go
back to my half-smile.

She doesn't mind; she ignores it. "Well…I brought
refreshments!" She pulls a bottle of champagne out of her bag.
I do laugh at this, and head into the kitchen for glasses.

It's been months since I've had anything to drink. While
we were trying to get pregnant, I stopped. I cried when the
nurse told me that I wasn't pregnant in the hospital. I only
cried to myself, not with anyone around. I didn't ask if she
could tell if I'd miscarried or just never was. *I don't want to*

*know.* I have an appointment with Dr. Patel in a couple of weeks. *Not that there's any point right now.*

Since Max hasn't even touched me. *Hell, he doesn't even sleep with me.* He sends me to bed each night and he doesn't come in. His side is cold and undisturbed each morning. I don't know if he sleeps in the guest room or the living room. He doesn't say and I don't ask.

Laura pours our glasses. "So…why aren't you at work today?"

"I decided to play hooky with my bff this afternoon." I smile and toast her for this. I think for one guilty moment about her being here without Max's permission. He came home briefly for lunch and said he'd be back for a late dinner. He only left one chore for me. "Rest." *Well, champagne can be restful…*

*Besides, I'll just write it down in the journal…won't matter anyway. He'd have to get close to me to punish me.* I down my glass and hand it to her to refill.

"Dang, girl. I'm going to have to keep up." She downs hers too. This feels good. It feels like old times.

"Have you talked to Tracy?"

She makes a face, but laughs. "Yes. She wanted to come too, but she has a big deadline." We both know that Max wouldn't have allowed this. I'm pretty sure the beefcakes outside have a list of who can and can't come in here. I wouldn't be surprised if she's on the do not allow list. "She sends you a hug though."

"Tell her that I'm not mad at her...or Rich...for their interviews. I know they were only trying to help me." Yesterday, I looked up blurbs online of the coverage from when I was missing.

Laura smiles at this and changes the subject. "So...seriously...can we get one of those guys to come in here and command them to do a striptease or something?" She fakes fanning her face.

"I'm pretty sure they're on strict orders to stay out..." I take another big gulp, feeling the effects already. "But, hell...after another drink...maybe we'll just have to try..."

Laura left about an hour ago. We drank the whole bottle and even opened another one. My head still feels fuzzy. I took a shower to try to clear it, but that just made me sleepy.

Max texted me that he won't be home for another hour. My rib is feeling a little better, so I try for a sexy bra and thong, leaving the wrap off. *Maybe if I just hang out in this in the bedroom...* Looking at myself in the mirror...*maybe not.* I'm still a giant bruise. I grab my robe just as the doorbell rings.

*It must be a pre-approved somebody because the dogs aren't barking.* This time, I laugh to myself. Laura actually did try to get them to come inside. *She's so bad! I hope they don't report that to Max...*

I open the door just holding my robe closed. I'm surprised. "Oh. Hi. He's not here."

"I know. He asked me to stop by…to stay with you until he gets home." Jake walks past me into the living room. *This is unusual… I already have two babysitters. And I've hardly seen Jake since…*

He takes a seat at the table, but I sit on the sofa. "So…he has something to talk to you about…?"

"No." He looks embarrassed. Then he drops the phony polite smile and he's just Jake, the friend I'd gotten to know over the months. Before all this. "He knows about my coming here, Lucy…to see you on Fridays."

I'm shocked. Max didn't say anything to me. I always assumed that if he ever found out, he'd be angry that I was keeping something from him. But I didn't want the visits to stop. It helped to talk to Jake. He was the only one who really understood what I said when I talked about Max, about us. He always helped me to see things from Max's side.

"He was pretty angry. So I was surprised when he called me this morning and asked if I was planning to see you today." I nod numbly. *Surprised is putting it mildly.* "I told him I wasn't. That I'd made that promise to him and I would keep it…" He looks embarrassed again.

I know Jake liked seeing me too. We didn't always talk about Max or my problems. I thought about him today at the usual time. I wondered if he'd come by. I was disappointed when he didn't. Seeing Laura in the afternoon helped, but it wasn't the same. I'd hoped that maybe it was the reason he waited to really see me, until we could be alone.

"Then he asked if I would, later though, closer to the time that he'd be home. He's bringing dinner with him a little later for the three of us." He continues to look embarrassed.

"Oh." It's all I can think to say. I'm still too tipsy and this is all too much.

Slowly through my haze, I realize I'm angry too though. *Max doesn't even say anything about my keeping this from him and then he just casually asks his brother to come see me himself?! I feel like I don't know him at all! We're worlds apart anymore!*

"Are you okay?" Jake looks a little concerned.

"I'm just tipsy…" I laugh at his exaggerated frown. *So like his brother.* "Yes. My friend dared to come into the inner sanctum and we drank some champers this afternoon…so sue me!" I'm angry with him too. *How quickly he threw away our friendship and now acts like a whipped puppy for his brother.* "In fact, I think I'll just have some more." I get up too quickly and spin a little on my toes heading towards the kitchen.

Jake follows and easily takes the bottle out of my hand. "Give me that. This is *my* house and I'll do what I want, Goddammit!" He upends the bottle into the sink. "Damn you! You have no right."

His look sends shivers up my back. *God how I wish Max would look at me like that again.* "Yes. I do. I'm here to keep an eye on you for Max. And you know better." *He even sounds like Max…or how he used to sound.*

"It doesn't matter."

"Why not? You don't care what Max thinks anymore?"

I shoot him what I hope is a deadly look, but I can feel my eyes crossing a little in the effort. I can hear myself slurring a little too. "*He* doesn't care anymore. Why should I?"

"Max cares, Lucy. You know he does. Why are you acting like this, getting drunk in the afternoon…shutting everybody out?"

I walk back into the living room. "I'm not shutting anybody out." I hiccup though. *Dammit.*

"Yes, you are. Max asked *me* to talk to you. Do you have any idea how hard that was for him?"

"I don't care." But I stop from sitting down on the sofa and turn to look at him. "He asked *you* to talk to me?" He nods. "About what?"

"About this. About why you're shutting him out. Ever since…" *He can't even say it. Goddammit! Coward!*

"You mean ever since I was *fucked* by another man?" And I flinch. Jake raised his hand like he was going to slap me, but he only ran it through his hair. But I saw that same flicker in his expression. *He wanted to slap me.*

"Watch your mouth, Lucy. You and I both know that Max doesn't let you talk like that. And I'm not going to stand here and listen to my brother's wife disrespect him."

I was shocked for only a moment. I bounce back to being pissed. I'm sobering up a little with anger. "Screw you. You were fine disrespecting him all those months you came over here. You think I'm going to listen to you now because you're acting like his errand boy, Jake?!" And I flinch again when he takes a step closer to me. This is not the same Jake I've known.

He only turns away for a second, takes two steps towards the terrace, then quickly comes back to stand close to me again. "You were hurt, Lucy. You went through something no one should ever have to go through." He looks me up and down. "But you're here. You're back where you belong. With Max. Why are you throwing that away, girl?"

"He's throwing me away! Why don't you ask *him* why?" I yell this at him. My throat cracks, I yell so loudly.

He only blinks at me. I keep staring at him, I don't back down. Jake's voice is calm and quiet when he answers, "He's worried about you. Don't you get that? He's afraid to do or say the wrong thing right now…"

"No. He's afraid to touch me. He doesn't *want* to touch me. Can you blame him?" Before I even realize what I'm doing, I throw off my robe. "*Look* at me? Would *you* want me?"

I didn't put my wraps or bandages back on after the shower. I stand in my barely there lacy bra and thong, my arms out for him to see every bruise, bump, gash, and slash.

Jake doesn't move, just looks me up and down very slowly. His breathing is fast and hard. He finally lowers his eyes and turns a little to the side. "Put your robe back on, Lucy."

I reach down and pull it up to cover my front, but I don't put it on. My voice is near tears. "Max doesn't want me anymore, Jake. He doesn't want a girl who will forever remind him…my *body* will forever remind him of what Ben did to me. A man like Max…he can't live with knowing that…that I won't be *his only* ever again…"

I move to get by him, but he grabs my arm and yanks me back to face him. "You don't think a man like Max would want you?" I only shake my head, too shocked to answer. His face is stern and angry; his grip cuts into my arm painfully. "I *am* just like Max. I've wanted you the moment I first saw you. In that bar. With that bruise on your face. I wanted to take you away from him. To protect you. To keep you." He shakes me and I wince from the pain to my side and arms. He gives me the same crooked grin that I love from Max. "But I didn't want to protect you from *me*. I wanted to have you all to myself. So *I'd* be the only one that could hurt you." He lets me go, shoving me back as he does. I stumble and drop my robe.

Now I feel very naked, I try to cover myself with my arms and pick it up again. "No." He grabs it out of my hand. "No. You want to show me. Then show me." He looks me up and down again. "You think a few cuts and broken bones would keep me away? You think seeing what another man did to you would matter to me?" He yells this. And I shake. Not out of fear, but longing. *I want to hear this. I need to hear this. But not from him. This is all wrong.*

I try to walk away again, but he grabs my arm and shoves me back further. "I didn't tell you you could go." He stares at me and I try to cover myself again. "I think you're more beautiful this way, Lucy. I'd keep you this way if you were mine." I can only stare at him. *I don't know this Jake.* He's never been anything but kind and gentle to me. I've seen hints of his darker side, but nothing like this. "Doesn't Max like seeing you beat up? Doesn't he get hard for you when you cry for him?"

"Please…stop…"

He throws my robe at me and I quickly put it on.

"We're not nice men, Lucy. If you think for a second that Max wouldn't do worse to you if he thought he could stop himself once he started…you're kidding yourself." He steps close to me again and I move a step back. "I *know* he'd love nothing more than to erase any memory of another man on you…but that would mean breaking you all over again." He moves back, takes a deep breath. "Is that what you want? Is that what you're doing? Pushing him, me…for what? So you have an excuse to leave?"

I lower my eyes and hold my robe tightly closed. In a tiny, faraway voice, "I'd never leave him, Jake." I ignore what he's said about wanting me…*I can't think of this now. Not now.*

Through gritted teeth, "Then you better figure out how to start behaving again. How to convince him of that."

My head is starting to spin. My stomach rolls. "I want him. But I can't be the one to reach out to him…that's not how we work."

"You'll have to find a way then…to make him see that you want things back the way they were…if that's even possible."

He turns to walk out to the terrace.

"Jake?" He turns around to look at me. "Did you only say all that...for Max?" I don't know what makes me ask...*maybe I need to know that at least one Traeger man would accept me as I am now...*

He comes back to stand in front of me, but this time he's more like the gentle Jake I know. "No." He puts his hands on my shoulders, gently, rubbing his hands down the back of my arms. He kisses the top of my head, taking a deep breath in. "I meant it. I've wanted you. I shouldn't have and I shouldn't have told you even now." He steps back and drops his hands. "I held myself back before. In every relationship, with every girl. I've not allowed my true feelings to direct my actions. I forced myself to toe a different line, not Dad's."

His look changes a little, back to a darker frown. "But while you were missing, I realized...what if I missed my chance at happiness? What if I missed my chance to tell you that what you have with my brother is exactly what I want to have...even if it can't be with you?" He walks away again, but stops at the open terrace door. Over his shoulder, not looking at me, "You're wrong about Max, Lucy. He's not holding back because he doesn't want you anymore. He's afraid to let go right now out of fear of what he'd do to you. I can sympathize."

I watch him sit on the sofa outside, his back is to me. Then I run to the bathroom and lose a lot of the champagne that's churning my stomach.

I sit on the marble floor and cry, the first real tears I've cried for myself in a while. I've cried from the pain. I've cried from the fear. But these tears are all for me...for how hopeless I feel.

*Nothing will ever be the same again. It only took ten days to ruin everything.*

My tears don't last long; even for myself, I'm too wiped out to stay anything but numb for long. I get up when I hear the front door open and close. I splash my face with cold water and stare in the mirror. I'm sick of looking at myself.

*I wish I could run Ben over again...maybe in my dreams tonight.*

## 65 Him

The bedroom door is closed. Jake's on the terrace. I drop the food in the kitchen and head out to him.

He doesn't say anything just gets up and stares at me. I frown and smile at the same time. My brother has become a mystery to me. I've not been able to figure out his looks, what's behind them exactly. He's always been so emotional, so mercurial, quick to flare up and just as quick to cool down. He's never been distant.

"So…did you talk to her?"

"Yes." He moves to walk by me, but I put my hand on his chest. He looks at my hand, then at me. I almost laugh. *Could swear he wants to hit me.* Instead he turns to face me. "She says she wants things back the way they were, but doesn't know if you do. She's waiting for *you* to do something." I let him walk inside this time.

*She wants things back to normal? Then why is she pushing me away?*

Jake heads down the hall to the door. "You're not staying for dinner?"

He doesn't turn around. "No. You two need time alone." Just before he opens the door though, he turns to face me. *He's angry*. Angrier than I've ever seen him before, but his voice is calm. "This makes us even, Max. Don't ever ask me to use my feelings for her to help you again." He closes the door quietly behind him.

I knew it was risky, asking Jake to come here today. He was here the day she went missing. *Behind my back. Their secret. I've not gotten over that.* I've had to bury my anger, wait for the right time.

Lucy needed someone to talk to. She isn't talking to me. For her sake, I would've turned to Tracy if I thought it would help. As much as it pisses me off, she obviously has something with Jake…an ability to talk to him about what she can't talk to me about. *I'd do anything to help her*.

He's right. I used him. I used the feelings I think he keeps hidden for her. For Lucy, I risked letting him get closer to her again. But I trusted him too.

And my risk paid off. He said she wants things back to normal…and that I need to do something to make that happen. *But I don't know that I can…not yet.*

I walk over to the bedroom door and quietly open it. Lucy is just closing the closet door, a dress in her hand. "Come out here." She looks at the dress, then me. "Now."

I don't wait to see if she follows. I just move into the living room. She quietly moves to sit on the sofa. "No. Stay standing." But there's something off about her eyes, the way she's moving. "Are you drunk?"

She tries to shake her head, but hiccups and puts her hand to her mouth. "No. Just a little tipsy. Laura came over this afternoon…"

"Did you ask me if she could be here today?"

"No…But she surprised me…"

"Is that an excuse? For breaking a rule?" She only shakes her head. "And then you make it worse by getting drunk? What the hell were you thinking?!"

"I wasn't thinking. I'm tired of thinking! I just wanted to have a nice day with a nice friend. So what? Do you really care?"

I raise my hand automatically. Lucy's never talked back, yelled back like this. But I stop myself. *Her face isn't even healed. I can't.*

She just shakes her head, still angry and tries to walk away.

"Get back here, Lucy."

She keeps walking. And I let her. I let her close the door to me. I let her push me away again.

All my anger…it's there, a caged animal growling to get out, to get at her. *But I can't open that door.*

Jake may think she's waiting for me to do something...*but I know that if I do, if I let the animal have her now...we'll never come back from that. I never will.*

I didn't picture just slapping her. I pictured breaking her lips open with my fist. I pictured her begging me to forgive her with blood on her mouth. I pictured grabbing her by her side and making her scream when her rib pops again while I squeeze. *I pictured my nightmares coming to life.*

I've held onto this rage and anger, this fear for too long. *If I let it go now...*

*I can't.*

I go into the guest room and quietly close the door.

*My Lucy is lost to me. I can't help her. I can't help myself. Not now. Not yet.*

*If I act now, I'll lose her forever.*

It's the only control I can take right now. Control of myself. Again.

**66** Her

I wait in the living room for Max to get home for lunch. I'm not calm, but all the crying I did earlier has helped to steady my nerves a little.

*My life has been so upside down, that I didn't think my nerves could take anymore. But I was wrong.*

Max hasn't slept in the same room with me in weeks. If he does, he sleeps on top of the sheets, turned away from me. He barely looks at me. And I stare at him.

I was hopeful, that maybe Jake would talk to him, that I'd find the courage to talk to him. But I said it to Jake. *That's not how we work.*

And we haven't been working. *I know now that…it's too late. We never will again. Not after today.*

I look at my suitcases sitting in the hallway. I said I'd never leave him, but I have no choice. He'll push me out the door. *When he finds out the truth... he won't ever be able to forgive me. What small chance there was for us anyway is gone now.*

I jump when the doorknob turns. *Take a breath! Stay calm!*

He comes in as usual. My handsome husband, he always takes my breath away when he's dressed in a suit. He's the picture of a powerful man.

He drops his bag on the table, right next to my suitcases.

I look down and wait. I have my speech in my head memorized, but I wait for him to make the first move. *I always do.*

But he doesn't say anything. He just walks by me into the bedroom. I hesitate. I don't know what I should do. *He saw the suitcases... but he didn't say anything at all?*

*He's not going to say anything?! This is it. I just leave? He...*

I start sobbing. My body is hit with great big sobs. I hold my stomach, my side. My rib still hurts and I try to press away the pain, but I can't stop sobbing.

*He doesn't even want to know why? He doesn't care at all...*

I stumble a little down the hallway, towards my bags. I try to breathe, but it's no use.

"Where do you think you're going, little girl?"

His voice stops my next shuttered sob. I turn around quickly. Max is leaning against the wall a few feet from me. His jacket is off; his shirtsleeves are rolled up.

I swallow and take a few quick breaths. I try to put my speech back in my mouth. "I…I need to…" more swallowing, my mouth is suddenly dry, my tears choked. *I don't want to say it. Please…* but I know I have to.

"What you need to do is unpack those bags." His voice is that same commanding voice he hasn't used in a long time. We've been ghosts around each other, barely talking at all for weeks, hardly in the same room together. *I miss his voice. His commands.*

*But it's too late for that.* I pull my shoulders back and swallow one big gulp of air. "I need to talk to you, Max."

He doesn't move. "I know what you need to say, Lucy." He glances at my bags behind me. "You went out this morning." *I should've known that his henchmen would be reporting everything to him.* I tried to get them to stay in the car, but they wouldn't leave me alone. Boss' orders. I only nod in response.

"Follow." He turns around and goes into the bedroom. And amazingly, I do. I'm his puppy still.

But I stop at the doorway. He goes to the closet and stands next to the opened door. The belt swings next to him, on its usual hook, unused and forgotten. "Hand me the belt, Lucy."

I shake my head. *It's too late for this.* "I need to tell you…" But I don't get this out. Max moves so quickly, I don't even see his hand as it grabs my throat, cutting off all words. He shoves me against the wall, slamming my head and body back, pinning me with his hand on my throat.

I put my hands up to his to try to pull it away. "Put your hands down." My eyes search his. The intensity of his anger makes me suddenly very frightened. Not just for me. *Oh God. He does know. And he's going to kill me?*

I push with all my strength against his chest, but he's a stone I can't budge. I feel my right wrist strain and cry out, as much as I can against his pressure on my throat. It's no use. I drop my hands.

"Please…Please just let me go…" It's all I can do. *He doesn't want me…maybe I can get him to see through his anger that letting me go is punishment enough.*

He laughs. It's a harsh, thick laugh. "Never, little girl."

He pulls me by my throat away from the wall and pushes me towards the bed, but he keeps his hand on my throat. "…Just let me go…please…"

He releases my throat and I cough, holding it myself and taking in big gulps. "You belong to me, Lucy. *All* of you belongs to me."

He moves quickly to the closet and grabs the belt himself. I bolt for the door before he turns around. I've never been as fast as him. He grabs my arm and swings me back around. I fall on the floor, sliding.

"You're not leaving this room without a beating, little girl."

*Is that what he wants? To punish me one final time? To show me that I mean nothing to him anymore?!*

"Get up and take off your clothes."

I hesitate. *Options*? I don't have any. He blocks the door.

I look up at him through my hair. He's calmer looking, but his eyes are fire still, his jaw is set, hands are fists, one with the belt. *He won't kill me. But he will hurt me.*

I stand, shaky, but I don't undress. "Why are you doing this?"

He slaps me with the back of his hand. The right side of my mouth explodes with pain and I can taste copper. I stagger back.

"I tell you to do something. You do it." But his voice is even; it's at odds with his tense body and eyes.

I watch myself, my hands. I'm numb. I push the front of my dress off my shoulders. I push myself out of the sleeves and see the dress pool at my feet. But I stop here.

"The rest." I look up at him. He has the same stern, but calm look. I take off my bra and thong. I put my hands protectively around myself. Then I look at him again. I dare him to hurt me with my look. I hope that staring him down will be enough. *He's backed away before. When I've pushed him. Maybe it's my only hope now. To not show fear.*

But I'm very afraid. *We've not been here, like this, in a long time. I don't know what he knows. I don't know how he'll react when he finds out the truth.*

He smiles his crooked grin. *The one I know so well... it always comes when he sees my pain. The pain he's caused.* I lose my nerve and hold myself a little tighter. But I don't look away. My eyes plead. His smile darkens.

"Did you really think I would let you leave?"

I only shake my head. Somewhere in my mind, I knew I would have to face his wrath first. Somewhere in my mind, I wanted this.

*To be broken. A clean break. Like Jake said.*

*I was a fool.*

## 67 Him

*I didn't know it, but today is what I've been waiting for, and I don't like to wait.*

I feel good, though, for the first time in weeks. Lucy's heartbeat against my hand. Her attempts to swallow and speak and breathe against my grip. Her look of pure fear. *God, I've missed you, little girl.*

I go for the belt. *It's time I teach her a good lesson in who her body belongs to once and for all.*

She tries to run. I take one second to laugh before grabbing her and yanking her back towards the bed.

She tries to stall, talk back. *Bad move, little girl.* I slap her. Not her left side, this is still too hurt. Her cheekbone is still healing. *But her right side…that's fair game.*

I watch her undress. *My Lucy*. I notice everything. It's been so long since she's stood in front of me nude. Every scratch, bite, scar. *All mine*. Her rib looks better, still swollen a little, still bruised. *Too bad. Not going to stop me. Not today.*

I'm the monster from my nightmares. But I'm in control of the animal. I have it on a leash. *But I can give it a little room to play...*

When I got the text asking if it was okay that Lucy was leaving the apartment this morning. I knew. I just knew where she was heading. In the back of my mind, I already knew what was going to happen.

I was calm, calmer than I've been in weeks. Every moment of anger and pain and fear was gone. It was replaced by a clear image. *Us. Lucy and me. Our future*. I've waited long enough. Given her more time than I should've. But it was for this moment. *Today. Our future starts all over again.*

This is what I've been waiting for. *To prove to her. To me. That we belong together no matter what.*

I wasn't surprised when I saw her bags packed. *She'd want to run. She doesn't believe in me anymore. But she will.*

I've questioned my ability to bring her back from her nightmares, to make her all mine again. I waited through her healing. *But I'm through questioning, waiting*. There's too much at risk.

"Did you really think I would let you leave?" She doesn't move, trying to look so brave. Her arms wrap around herself. *Good*. "Did you think I'd let you leave with our baby inside you?"

Her eyes widen with fear. She shakes her head and almost apologetically whispers, "It's not yours." *I know this already.* I talked to her doctor after she left her office this morning. The timeline matches with Lucy's disappearance. There's only a small chance that the baby she's carrying is mine. *I don't care. Boy or girl, it's* mine. *Ours.*

I move quickly, grabbing her throat again. "I own all of you, little girl." I shake her and squeeze harder before shoving her onto the bed. I get on top of her before she can move, pinning her hands under me. I squeeze her side with my legs and she gasps from the pain to her ribs. I slap her right side again. Harder this time. I won't leave a bruise. *Not this time. Plenty of time for that.*

"Don't you get that?" She shakes her head, tears of fear and pain start, her beautiful blue eyes are bright with both. *God, she makes me so hard.* "*You* are mine. Everything about you is mine, including this baby." I run my hand over her face, from the left side down to her throat, across to her right rib. "You think you'll ever be anything except mine? You think what he did to you makes a difference? That you can push me away?"

She shakes her head uncontrollably, sobbing loudly. I slap her again. And again. *Maybe I will bruise her. Give her something else to see in the mirror.* But I stop myself. *Not today.* I have something else in mind for her today.

I get up, pulling her with me, off the bed. I hold onto her arm and pull her against me. "Look at me."

She does, but her eyes are wild with fear and tears. And longing. *My sweet Lucy.* I pull her close and smash her lips with mine. Her tongue is eager, searching my mouth, licking the back of my teeth, the roof of my mouth. I taste her copperiness. *Good. It's a start.*

I pull her away and my sweet hungry Lucy moans. "I'm never letting you go again. You will never be left alone. You will never be anywhere but where I tell you to be. Do you understand me, little girl?"

"Yes, Sir." *So eager.*

I put my hand on her lower belly, holding her against me. She puts her hands over mine, instinctively protective. *Good.* After I talked to her doctor, I'd worried that Lucy was thinking that she could end this pregnancy. That she might not want this baby. "This *is* mine. Have no doubt in your head, little girl, that you and this baby belong to me. Only me." She only nods. "Say it!"

"I belong to you." She swallows. "My baby belongs to you." But this is too much for her. She wails a big cry. Jerking against my hold on her arm, she throws herself into my other arm.

I drop the belt and hold her, squeezing her to my chest, holding her head against me. I can't understand what she says, it's a jumble of tears and stuttered words. I just hold her and rub her back. I soothe her with whispers and kisses. It's been too long since I've held her like this.

She finally starts to quiet, sobs turn to only tears and hiccups. I walk her back to the bed and sit with her on my lap. Her arms still clutch around my neck.

I speak softly into her hair, still rubbing her back and leg. "Did you really think I wouldn't want you? That I'd let you just walk out of here?" She only shakes, no words. I lift her chin up. "I failed you." She starts to open her mouth. "No. Just listen. I know that I failed you. I let you get hurt. It was my job to protect you and I didn't. I'll always be sorry for that, baby." She rubs against my hand. *My good girl.*

"I know that you're strong. Stronger than anyone I've ever met. You're strong enough to take all of me...all of my demands, all of my anger. I know you don't *need* me, Lucy. You proved that. You got away from that asshole on your own." I stop.

I don't know if I should say the rest, but I know she needs to hear it. She needs to understand that I understand. She lost her faith in me, but I never lost my faith in her. "I've heard you crying at night. I've heard your nightmares. But I know that whatever he did to you...that you're still my sweet Lucy. You weren't broken by it, little girl. I know you can take care of yourself no matter what...but *I* need *you.* I need you to love me." Her hands go to my face. I kiss her palm and she smiles her sweetest smile. *My Lucy.*

"I almost failed you again...giving you too much space the past few weeks. I was waiting until you were healed completely..." I let some of the anger I've felt creep back into my eyes and voice. "I thought that's what you needed. I thought you needed time to come back to me on your own. But I know that you won't be fully healed until I make you mine again." She only nods. Her look of fear and guilt is back. It's that perfect combination that shoots straight to my cock and pushes all rational thought aside. But I hold back a little longer.

"I don't care how you're pregnant, Lucy. This *is* my child. *Our* child. I was raised by a man who wasn't my father.

But I've only ever had one dad." She nods again, tears slip out of her eyes, a small smile crosses her lips. I put my hand on her stomach again. "You were born for me. And this child will be born for us." She kisses me, a gentle, tender kiss.

"I love you, Max."

"And I love you." I kiss her back with a little more force. I can feel my cock hard under her. *I've waited too long to have what's mine again.*

I pick her up and set her on her feet. "Bring me the belt, Lucy." She blinks, fear back. *Good.*

She puts her hand on her stomach. I laugh, but manage to keep my face stern, shaking my head, "That's not going to save you, little girl. You have a punishment coming. And you can take it." She moves slowly to the belt on the floor and picks it up. She brings it back to me slowly too. I love watching her move, her little walk back, one foot in front of the other, almost on tip-toe.

I like the feel of the belt in my hand, the weight. I shift it around so the buckle hangs loose a little. She stares at my hand, eyes wide. She's beautiful. *I've missed this.*

I look her up and down. Her wrist is swelling again, so is her side near her ribs. For this punishment, she can't lie down; she can't hold her weight against a wall or bed either. I stand and put my left arm out in front of her, across her chest, holding her upper right arm with my hand. "Brace yourself against my arm." She figures out what I mean, moving her hands to cup under and over my arm, pressing herself against my strong hold.

She lowers her head, her hair tickles over my arm and her hands. I lean her forward a little, not quite on tip-toe. "Arch your ass in the air, little girl. Show me you want this." She does. I feel my cock throb looking at her. Her chest thumps and breath quakes against my arm.

"I'm going to hit you with the buckle." She shudders, but I keep her still. "Only on your bottom." Her second shudder is a little less. *Good*. She grips my arm more. "Take a deep breath in." She does. I know with her rib hurting, I'll have to go slow, allow her time to catch her breath. *I don't mind. The animal on the leash does...but I'll like making this last.*

I let the first strike hit just as she ends her deep breath out. She screams and dances on my arm. I like the intimacy. *I may have to spank her in this position more often.* I can feel her every reaction. I wait for her to calm, her breath to catch, her body to stop shaking. I hit her again, only a little harder, still on the plumpest part of her ass. Same scream, same dance. Her body heats against me.

I wait again, giving her a little more time. I watch as her ass shows two perfect buckle prints. Bright red. I hit harder. She screams a little louder. One more, same spot. Same scream.

"Do you think you've had enough, little girl?" This is a special part of this particular punishment.

"Please…"

"That's not an answer." I hit her hard again, close to the last one. Her yelp is a gulp for tears and air.

"Yes." She gasps for air, "Yes, Sir."

"No. You don't decide when you've had enough." I hit her again, not as hard. "Have you had enough, little girl?"

"Please…I don't…" She cries and sobs against my arm, her head rocking up and down. *My beautiful Lucy*. Her ass a tight plaid of buckle marks on her round cheeks. I hit her again, still not as hard. The buckle is leaving a deep red mark. *I want to see this on her thighs too, but I already said I'd limit it to her ass. Next time…when she deserves a harsh punishment again.*

"Have you had enough?" I wait with the belt ready.

"Only if you say so." She's quick with this answer. It's a single word almost, carried with her breath in. I want to laugh and tell her she's a good girl. *Not yet. She has another lesson.*

"Good." She lets a long breath out with relief. *Almost cruel to make her think I'm through with her…almost.* "You kept a secret from me, little girl." She stiffens again. "What was it?"

"I…I'm sorry…I saw Jake…he'd come over…I'm sorry." She's sobbing again. I hit her hard to add to her tears. She screams and shakes again. I hit her once more hard before giving her a chance to breathe. I let her sobs run their course. I pull her up to stand straight, but don't let go. She's still too shaky. She clings to my arm.

I turn her to face me. Her face is all blotched, lashes wet with tears. *So beautiful*. "He won't be coming here anymore without my permission." She nods quickly. "You keep a secret from me again, little girl, and you'll feel this buckle on your back."

"Yes, Sir! Thank you, Sir!"

I let go of her arm, running my hand up to her shoulder, around her neck, to cup the back of her head. She's warm from her punishment. Her eyes take on that soft, half-opened look of hers. Lips part in want and need. I pull her towards me for the kiss. But keep it soft, feathering her lips with mine, running my tongue across the inside of her lips before feeling deeper.

She moans softly and I'm undone. I pick her up gently; her arms circle around my neck; her lips touch everywhere they can reach. I lay her gently on the bed, kissing her as she strains to keep our lips together, but I pull away. I take off my clothes quickly. It's been too long.

Her legs are open before I'm on the bed. I smile at my Lucy. *Mine again. Always.*

Entering her is everything. The warm, wet strength of her pull, her legs shake with the energy of forcing me in deeper. I let her control me for a moment. She squeezes and moans, arching her back and head, pulling on my shoulders, lifting herself off the bed to meet me more. It's almost more than I can take.

I push her back down with a firm hand on her chest. Her eyes pop open in surprise. *My turn.*

I grab her legs and bend them back, pushing into her deeper and harder. She puts her hands behind her head. "Good girl." She smiles. I can barely speak, trying to concentrate on making this last. *Oh, hell...* I give up and just fuck her hard and fast a few more strokes before I'm lost in my own deep moans.

When I look down, she's smiling at me, hands reaching for my neck. I lean down to give her a kiss, but she whispers in my ear, "You owe me one still..." She kisses my cheek and pushes her hips up and down, grinding against me again.

I grin. *Not a problem.* I'm getting hard again just feeling her squeeze me.

*I'm always ready for more of my Lucy.*

In the dark, holding her against my chest, hearing her little moans, soothing them away with my hand on her back, I know she's mine again. And I know that I'm hers. My heart will never heal from the ten days she was missing...I'll never forgive myself. But she forgives me. She loves me. She's given me everything I've ever wanted, ever needed...her.

Control is about choices. And I never had any.

I didn't choose to fall for her. I just did.

I didn't choose to give her everything I am. I just had to.

I didn't choose to let fate step in our way. It just did.

I have no choice in how I love her. I just do.

I am a monster. And she just loves me.

Always.

The **alternate** ending for Max and Lucy can be read in

*True Control* 4.2.